A Place of

Tranquility

Lollie

Copyright © 2012

All rights reserved.

ISBN:1499701683

ISBN-13:9781499701685

Content in Grace

When he married his wife, Nicholas O'Ryan prophesied of new memories for Park, thus pushing the thoughts of little Mary Ann Livingston, and the torments of her soul, back into the safe crevices of forgetfulness as Park Stevens O'Ryan emerged permanently victorious.

Remnants of that little girl victim, that victim that was so distorted inside and out, could finally be buried. All the roots and fingerlings of that dark shadow could be removed. Mary Ann Livingston metamorphosed when she came of age into the identity of Park in order to erase the past horrors forever. However, per his nature, Satan ran to and fro, seeking whom he may devour.

He slammed the painful reminder of who she was. In the process, destroying that strong willed being she once had been. It would take a lot longer for her to expunge it once again. Fortunately, Nicholas aided her in this desperate endeavor.

With the help of her new husband, she was successful in doing this. Seldom came any remembrance of the old life, except when her youngest daughter imitated a mannerism that reminded her of her husband that had gone Home way too soon. Her dear Matt would always hold that spot so dear in her heart that none could touch. He and their best friend, Bruce, had helped her survive childhood. He had served his country, until he was taken prisoner and killed in the line of duty.

No, no one could ever replace Matt, but Nicholas found a way into her heart and the two shared a love that surpassed any she had ever known.

Their jobs as secret agents benefited from the union of this vibrant team. Their personal connection caused a tighter bond as they seemed untouchable. They were no longer two people, but one entity known as 'Nick-n-Park'.

The small family quietly celebrated the first wedding anniversary of their marriage aboard the gifted sea vessel, *Freedom's Park*. Park O'Ryan praised God for his blessings in letting her find two loves of this nature in one lifetime.

Their lives seemed to be falling into fairy tale status. Things were going too well. Park did not feel she deserved to be this happy and content. If her past dictated anything at all, she knew it would be short lived.

As the fall season came, Nicholas's sister's family came to Charleston to begin a new tradition for Thanksgiving. Because of this, Park and Nicholas added an apartment over the garage for the extended family. They wanted to provide them a home away from home.

Kathy was grateful to see her father looking younger these days. She knew the move was good for him. Finding her long lost brother had been a blessing. She was beginning to doubt that her lovable old dad would ever move back to Kansas.

Another annual fall tradition was the POW benefit, which Grant Grayson began in search of his MIA son. He had the good fortune of finding his son, Shawn, a few years earlier on one of his rescue missions, and bringing him home.

However, this year they were without their founder. Sadly, he had died, leaving Shawn acting as the man in charge. He bore the years of prison camp with dignity.

Semi retired from the Air Force, Park agreed to a few consignments. This partnered her with her oldest and best friend, Bruce, once again. Mostly, what they did was test pilot new planes and equipment. She enjoyed doing this, until one day she almost shot down Bruce's plane and he tormented her unmercifully about trying to kill him.

Life seemed to be going pleasantly for a woman that had endured very little pleasure in her existence. She began attaining a routine of sorts, and grew complacent in her newfound joy.

Chameleon

Summer arrived vigorously on South Carolina that year, so Pop, as Park so lovingly called Nicholas's dad, took their two daughters to spend their summer vacation in Kansas with Kathy's family, after Sarah celebrated her birthday.

Then, death knocked at Bruce's door. His ailing dad made his final journey. Park was glad he had found love again with Christy. She seemed to be a balm for his grief. The funeral exposed a large loving family that seemed to leave Bruce in the cold. It was no wonder that he had turned to that little pip-squeak girl for companionship, when they were kids. Her heart ached for her friend.

Consequently, the O'Ryans was not able to finish the trip because duty called. A sly terrorist had evaded the FBI for months. He managed to escape before capture every time, as if he were always one step ahead of them. It was time for the agency to put their best men on the job.

The fiend was Gorshev, and he had claimed responsibility for the deaths of a hundred and thirty-four, men, women, and children in a bombing in the small country of Yakistan. Chasing after him would not render the result of capture any sooner, so they decided to decipher where his next plan of attack would be to gain advantage of him.

Several FBI agents had not returned from their assignments. Hopeful, that in finding Gorshev, they would find the MIA operatives as well.

Rumors had it that he was in search of chemical warfare from a small time black marketer, Enrique, in the low key Marseille, France. Enrique had been a student activist, revolting against the common diplomacy of his country, which made him a fugitive and forced him underground. He had low funds and primitive supplies, but he had seized a scientist who had discovered the formula for this specific chemical.

Enrique was renowned for recruiting people from his old college, so their boss, Richardson, started there by enrolling Park as a college student. She appeared youthful, and with the proper attire, she could pass as a student.

They gave her a background of a girl who had lost her brother in the IRA's civil hostility. Her father spent time in the Irish jail systems, after the authorities suspected him for being a part of the militia. This gave her the reason to be angry with the government, therefore, attractive to Enrique for enlistment.

His modus of operandi was to show up at rallies or protests to scope for new recruits. This is where he found his next victim. Park, also known as Patty, sat in the sidelines watching the whole rioting.

Enrique took notice of her beauty before he took notice of her rebellion. He approached her as a conquest for love, not a recruit for his plots.

"Are you enjoying the festivities?" he asked.

"Festivities?" she responded in full Irish tongue,

"This is nothing compared to where I come from."

"Where are you from, Mademoiselle?"

"Ireland, proud and true. You are French?"

"Marseille, proud and true as well."

She lifted her hand to shield the sun from her eyes and smiled, "I do not remember seeing you around the campus, did you just transfer?"

"No, I finished a long time ago. I just come every now and then to see if anything ever changes. Of course, it never does." He tried not to accentuate his French, to no avail. The tongue rolled the French accent fluently.

"What do you think of the riots, Mr..."

"Enrique. Philippe Enrique. May I have the pleasure of making your acquaintance?"

"Patty O'Brien. The pleasure is all mine," she smiled the charm that one could not resist. He swallowed the bait.

9

Enrique

"The riots are not going to make these pigs listen. They must take some action. Our government will never sit down for negotiations," he was saying.

Patty grimaced, "I understand what you mean. In our country, they arrest citizens for mere suspicion of treason. My father served their prisons for four and a half years because they saw him give bread to a beggar, who happened to be the mother of a militant. They would not listen to him that he knew not of the IRA. They carried him to prison without a trial."

"The pigs! I should like to destroy that government," Enrique pried for more. He thought he might have a new recruit as well as a love interest here. With looks like hers and a proper hatred for the government, she could be a lethal weapon herself. Yet, he would have to have her checked out, before he revealed himself as a radical.

"I plan to," she gritted with hatred in her voice, "I will join the militia when I finish school, and we will make our government regret having ever thrown my father in jail." Acting as if she said too much to this stranger, she shut her lips tight, trying to ignore him.

"My respects to a fellow comrade, and a very charming one, I might add. I will see you at tomorrow's demonstration, no?"

"I must really stay at school and finish. The sooner I graduate, the sooner I can help my father." She stood to leave.

"What is the mademoiselle majoring in?"

"I am going to be a lawyer, so I can pay retribution for my father, but I am majoring in Political Science for now. Later, I go to England for my law school."

The French man was kissing her hand goodbye, "I do hope to meet you again, Mon Cherie." He went straight to his warehouse to begin the search on the Irish beauty. He handed her name over to his man to search her background thoroughly.

The process of an intensive search for the criminal mind of Enrique took two days. He had hoped to see the lovely mademoiselle at the demonstration the next day, but was disappointed. Park decided that she should not just all of a sudden appear at all the riots going on, since she never had been to one of them.

Enrique appreciated her exhibition of refusing to get in the limelight for 'the cause'. This showed discipline. If she could remain discreet while being underhanded, this would be a treasure to the cause. He searched her whereabouts throughout the campus, asking one student or another, "Where would the Political Science classes be?" or "Have you seen Patty O'Brien?" until he found her the third day.

The professor caught sight of the renowned criminal talking to his new student and openly advised Patty not to associate with this bum.

Enrique glared at him, while Patty just smiled and said, "It is all right. I know what I am doing."

Her response put a smile on the wicked face, "Come Cherie, I have something to show you."

He took her to the warehouse, which doubled for lab, office, and all. He carefully explained his 'cause' while scrutinizing her for a reaction. Pleased with what he saw, he continued to demonstrate his plans.

When he questioned her as to whether she would be interested in joining his league, she hesitantly asked him about finishing college. He told her he wanted her to finish. He could use a crooked lawyer down the road. She haltingly agreed to it.

He showed her the lab where a kidnapped scientist was producing some more of the chemical weaponry as demanded. The professor looked at the newcomer with a pleading in his eyes, yet he dared not speak.

Enrique explained his plan to sell the chemicals to

make more money for the cause. He had a buyer that wanted a hundred and seventy-five grams by seven o'clock Tuesday night. He wanted that to be Patty's début. Acting like the nervous girl, she was supposed to be, Park agreed with the assurance in her heart, that the buyer was Gorshev.

   She went to classes daily, as well as Enrique's warehouse, to legitimize authenticity of learning what to do. Meanwhile, she contacted Richardson about the meeting, who informed her that she would be alone on this one. Her cover would not allow Nicholas an entry. She was to tag Gorshev and get out. The parameters were set.

Compound Interest

Gorshev did not get where he was on the terrorist scale by having his head turned by a pretty face and was not cordial to Patty's presence. He reluctantly did his business by way of this extra witness, and immediately withdrew.

"What an adrenaline rush!" exclaimed Patty, returning from the meet. "What do we do now?"

"Well love, you go back to school and wait for the news to report fireworks. Drop by in a few and we'll talk."

After the successful mission, Park did not go back to the college. She met up with her team to proceed. The tracing led them to follow Gorshev to Kiev, Ukraine. Another team was to meet them en route for backup.

Finding the abandoned military base, where Gorshev was located, proved to be the easiest part. Getting inside the compound was more difficult. They were able to crawl through the sewer lines that ran underneath, which led them to the outside of the old cafeteria.

The team split up in order to explore options. Gorshev had a slew of men under his leadership who would lay down their lives for their commander.

Guards loomed everywhere and almost caught Park. There was no communication between agents for fear of someone overhearing. If captured, she was on her own.

Nicholas was the first to find entrance. Another agent, Sparks followed his lead. He signaled the rest of his team to cover the outside.

The remaining eight-team members listened and watched under the cover of the night. Uneasiness settled over the team in the long silence.

"I am in the outer layer of the computer room. Spark's, find where they have stored the chemical." The team heard Nicholas report in a quiet voice.

Silence, once more, filled the air. The few minutes

that passed seemed like hours to those who were waiting. Night had wrapped her black robe around them, making it near impossible to see. Lights were scarce, and Park began getting nervous. She had an uneasiness about her.

She did not like the idea of them possibly seeing her while she could see nothing. It stifled her breath. She wished Nicholas would hurry. Something in the air did not feel right.

It wasn't Sparks or Nicholas that they heard next. "What you doing here?"

They had caught Sparks! "Abort!" he called.

"Move in," ordered Nicholas.

Gunfire commenced with the entire team running into the compound.

"Set the charges, blow it," came the orders from Richardson through the communications devices they were wearing. "With those chemicals, she is going to blow hard. You have five minutes after detonation to get out. Park, take care of Gorshev."

Park searched for the computer room, thinking that was where Gorshev would be. "O'Ryan, location? Nicholas, where are you?" Silence was her answer. The computer room was full of men, but none was Gorshev. She certainly had to eliminate him. They couldn't risk him escaping the explosion and running free.

Park heard Nicholas, "Gorshev is on the second floor east section. I will take him. Get out, Park." A gunshot rang in the communication devices. Park retreated.

"Are you in egress, Nicholas?" Silence. "Nicholas, are you with me?" she turned on heels. Something was wrong. She bounded the steps to the second story two at a time. "O'Ryan, can you hear me? Nicholas, answer me." Nothing.

She ran to the south door to cross over to the east wing. Gorshev stood there with three other men. If Gorshev was here, then where was Nicholas? Had he been the one shot? She definitely heard a shot.

18

It was nothing for this trained agent to put the three men out of commission, but Gorshev ran as soon as his first man went down. Park caught sight of him going in the stairwell at the end of the hall. She ran, for her life did depend on it.

He went down. She descended half way and jumped over the rail to the next set of stairs. This she repeated again to get on the ground floor. She was only a beat away from him now. "Gorshev!" She commanded, placing a bullet in his shoulder to make him aware of her closeness.

Holding his wound, he turned to face her. "You are the woman that stupid Enrique has working for him. You double-cross him. I knew you were not to be trusted, you stupid woman."

"Where is the man you captured?"

"Both are dead." Her reaction betrayed her.

"Both? There were two?" Park needed to make sure

he said two. She repeated, "Two men?"

"You are going to kill me? Do it now!" he ordered.
His Russian accent was strong.

Vengeance is Mine

Richardson heard the conversation. "Park, everyone is accounted for except Sparks and Nicholas. He is gone. Drop Gorshev! Detonation time is two minutes and thirty-two seconds. Do it and get out!"

All the rage from thirty-two years surfaced inside this woman. She had not heard Richardson's order. All the torment she had suffered had come to claim victory over her, and she held nothing back of her anger as she shot Gorshev. Her whole body filled with vile hatred. She was glad to end his life, since he had so carelessly ended Nicholas's life. She did not stop shooting, until the gun clicked repeatedly.

She had to find her love. She could not leave without him. She climbed back up the stairs to where she first spotted Gorshev.

"O'Ryan hasn't come out yet!" Collins reported over the communication device. "Everyone else has cleared."

The widow ignored Richardson's order. "You have less than two minutes, Park. I order you to get out!" He waited for a response, but received none. "Collins, drag her out. Park, Nick is gone. It is too late for him. You need to get out."

Collins did not need Richardson to give the order. He was already ten seconds into his rescue when the boss gave him the orders. He saw movement on the balcony above where he entered the building. "Park!" he called out.

The figure stopped briefly. "Get out Collins. I am not leaving without Nicholas."

He ran the steps three at a time and followed her around a pillar. He saw her down the way and ran to her. Throwing her over his shoulder with a fight, he retraced his steps to exit. The two were only a few yards away when the old military base exploded, blowing the two of them a distance from the impact.

Park walked into the doors of the headquarters burdened with sorrow. They had blown her light out. Fred did not try to comfort her. He had been like a surrogate dad to her and now, he was at a loss. How could he comfort a twice widowed Precious?

It was a pointless ritual of debriefing, because she heard nothing and offered nothing in return. All of the grief she had felt when Matt died resurfaced. Her beloved Nicholas was gone. He would never be there to comfort her again. She wanted to die.

Richardson remained after everyone else left. "Park, I know what Nicholas meant to you. Words do not seem fit to express my sorrow. I will truly miss him. He was a good agent. He knew the risks, and you know this is the way he wanted it."

Park could not respond. Her lips had invisible thread, which had sown them shut. "Take me now, God. Please, take me now," her brain kept repeating. Her happiness had come to a sudden halt and ceased to exist. She was a cursed woman. It was as simple as that. She was destined to spend her life in misery, and anyone who dared love her would die. Why could she not just die herself, and end it all? Nicholas was gone. They were only married a year and a half, and now she was without completion once more. She did not hear Richardson's words or notice that he had left. Disbelief ran rampant in her heart. He could not be gone, because he promised to protect her from bad things like this.

She ended up at her house without even knowing how she got there. The house was still empty of children and Pop, for they were not due home for two more weeks.

She lay in a hot bath until chills overtook her. She found his shirt in the closet and put it on her cold aching body in hopes it would bring him back to her. Her heart was broken. Loneliness held its grip on her soul and refused it leniency.

Fred went by, but Park did not hear his knock. A few days later, he tried again under the pretense of inquiring about funeral arrangements. He found her house quiet and dark, and she still refused to answer the ringing bell.

He thought of the one person that would know how she was. Bruce greeted him with surprise when he appeared at the base. "Fred, old fellow, how are you?"

"Oh, I can't complain. You?"

"Fine sir, fine. What brings you out to our neck of the woods?"

Fred twiddled with his hat in his hands, "I came by to see if Precious is okay."

Bruce laughed, "Why wouldn't she be?"

Fred realized he was bearing the sad news to this friend. "Didn't she tell you?"

"Tell me what?"

"About Nick? He was killed during their last mission."

The expression withdrew from Bruce's face. His mouth gaped. "No, I thought she was still on assignment. I haven't heard anything from her. Is she at home?"

"I just came from there, but she won't answer the door. Her Jeep is still in the garage at work. I thought you might know where she is."

"Let's go," he flung to Fred.

He called Christy to meet him at Park's house post haste where he would explain. Thinking his old friend was in danger, he was there before his wife. His key to her house was in his hand before the car stopped.

"Check around downstairs and see if she left a sign of where she might have disappeared to. I'll check upstairs. Look for flight or taxi numbers, anything." His last words were cast down the stairs behind him." He burst into her bedroom, "Fred! She is here."

Fred was by his side in no time. She looked dead, lying stiffly in her bed. "Is she... still breathing?"

Heartbroken

"Yes. Park, Sweetie, wake up. Park O'Ryan, you better wake up now and tell me what is wrong."

"Anything?" breathed Fred.

"No. Dr. William Kendall is her doctor. Call him. He will come. Park, can you hear me?"

She tossed her head to the other side murmuring, "It hurts Nicholas. Please make it stop."

"Park, honey it is me, Bruce. Wake up."

She looked at his contorted form. She saw her Nicholas. See, he was not dead, so why was her heart literally breaking? She could not breathe because the pain was excruciating. She needed him to hold her now. "Nick…I love you so much. Don't leave me."

"Park, look at me. Nick is not here. Can you hear

me?" She fell into oblivion again. Bruce put a cool cloth on her burning forehead.

Dr. Kendall arrived with his medical bag in tow. He looked her over, and listened to her heart. "How long has she been this way?" he asked.

"We don't know," confessed Bruce. "When did she come home, Fred?"

"She left headquarters Friday morning."

"She needs to go to the hospital for some tests. It sounds like her heart may have committed some infraction. Her fever is outrageous, and we do not know how long it has been this high. She needs these tests in order for a proper diagnosis. I'll need her husband there to sign the permission papers for her, where is he?"

"Killed," this from Fred.

"When did this happen?" inquired the doctor.

Fred responded, "Thursday night."

The doctor turned immediately to phone an ambulance. "I can't believe you people left her here five days in this condition. I bet she has not had as much as a drink of water in days."

Christy had come in right after the doctor had and heard the news of her friend. She gathered a few personal belongings of Park's to take to the hospital. With Nicholas dead, they still needed permission forms signed from next of kin, so she called Albert McCrain, who immediately flew home.

Dr. Kendall found the anxious friends and family in the waiting room. "She is going to be fine. You can all stop worrying now. Her fever is down. She has an I.V. replenishing her dehydration. We may let her go home tomorrow."

"What about her heart?" asked Bruce.

"Her heart is weak. It has strained itself into constriction. There is no blockage. The heart has a diastole with each cardiac cycle, in other words, each beat

29

is a contraction and a relaxation. This completes a cycle. If the heart is strained, it does not relax, exhausting the muscle. The strain caused her to go into cardiac arrest. It was not serious enough to do much damage, but next time she may not be so lucky."

Christy held her husband's arm, "Is she in danger of having another attack?"

"If she is overstressed, yes, she is apt to have another. She has to get complete rest, and she has to eat properly. I will not release her until I know someone will take responsibility for her."

"I will do that," said Pop withdrawing from the corner. "I will be responsible for her."

"We all will, won't we Fred?" The small group huddled together in one accord to aid their loved one.

Albert McCrain had little time to mourn for his son, who was dead to him a second time. There needed to be a funeral and that little girl up in the bed would not be ready any time soon for this job.

He called Kathy in Kansas. He dreaded telling the girls. He knew Nick was not their biological father, but he was the only father Anna had ever known. Sarah had been through this before. How would she deal with it again?

The old lines burrowed into his brow again. Kathy would be in tomorrow and could help him make arrangements.

Bruce insisted that Mr. McCrain spend the night at his house, so the father would not have to grieve for his son alone. It gave them the opportunity to discuss plans. They decided that the best way to tell the girls about their dad would be for Bruce and Pop to tell them before Park came home. They would also have to tell them about their mom, so they could be careful not to upset her.

Convictions

Park was angry with herself for falling apart. She was embarrassed to have them bring her to the hospital and to be the topic of conversation. She simply wanted to be alone. Something inside of her refused to believe that Nicholas was dead. She would feel it in her soul if he were.

Everyone allowed her the solitude she desired. They quietly scurried around downstairs, leaving her to mourn in peace.

She caressed his pillow, smelling his scent. "Oh God," she cried, "Why could it not have been me?"

Christy and Kathy took care of the children. Pop wandered from room to room in a daze while Bruce and Fred returned to work. Together, the family prepared a memorial for their beloved.

Park sat through the memorial without hearing a

word or shedding a tear. Instead, she contemplated going back to Kiev to dig through the rubble and find proof he was not dead. It was a different feeling than when Matt died.

In the midst of the service, a strange conviction came upon this double widow. She became convicted of the hatred she felt for the man she killed. She murdered him to avenge Nicholas not because it was protocol. She committed the sin of murder. She had killed in her job before, but it was never a willing malicious act.

Though convicted, she refused to ask forgiveness, because her heart did not want to cease hating the fiend who ripped her soul from her. Anger at Almighty God for twice having taken her husband set deep in her heart.

She became the epitome of desolation. God promised He would never leave her nor forsake her, yet His presence was gone. He had taken Matt, and she tried to understand that it was God's will. Now, He had taken Nicholas, and that, she did not understand. What more could God want from her? All she had left to give was her

33

children, and He had even taken one of them. Where was God now that she needed Him for a Comforter?

Her hatred toward that man, whose life she traded for Nicholas's, was blinding her to the omnipresence of the Almighty Hand, which contained her bitter heart in its palm. He had not left her forsaken. Instead, she had stopped looking for Him. Deep from within her heart, she was angry with her Creator for this tragedy. The trials faced, heretofore, she faced with His grace. By her own act of rebellion, she had stepped outside of God's grace for this trial and had already failed.

"Pop," she said in a small voice one day, "I think I will go to Montana for a while."

"Do you want us to come, Little Girl? If you'd prefer, we'll stay here."

"I always want you with me," she smiled a pitiful smile, void of its former charm.

Pop was relieved to hear her answer. He did not

intend to let his little girl go off alone to make herself sick again, so he helped Sarah and Anna pack, and they were ready to fly the next morning.

Pop called Christy and Fred with her scheduled plans to travel, so they would not worry over her disappearance.

Coming to Grips

The grandgirls showed Grandpa all their little places of pleasure in their Montana getaway. He eyed Park cautiously, as she stared out over the lake. "She must still be in shock, poor little girl," he thought to himself.

Day after day, she would fulfill her motherly duties, and then retreat to the boat by the lake alone. The flowers that bloomed just for her went unnoticed. Day after day, she would sit and stare without speaking.

Other than the disruption of eating the meals Pop prepared, the heartbroken mother sat entranced. Tears still failed to come to her weary eyes. She had not cried at all since Nicholas died. He noticed on occasion that she would hold her heart as if it were breaking, until he could not stand it any more. He did not only lose a son; he lost a daughter, for she was dead inside.

After sending the girls to play, he ventured to her refuge. He could no longer watch her dwindle to nothing.

"Little girl, I am worried about you."

She did not answer immediately. He was almost ready to leave when she spoke, "Don't worry about me. Don't you know that I am made of steel? Nothing can hurt me."

He heard her bitterness. "You *are* hurting, and you won't let anyone help you."

"No one can help me," she retaliated venomously.

"I don't pretend to know much about God, but I know my son did, and you do too. I know you believe that He will help you when no one else can."

"And what if God is punishing me for being a horrid creature? What if it is His desire I suffer throughout eternity? It is not a matter of believing God. It is a matter of *why* He let it happen." She moved her hand to her heart again.

Pop noticed a subtle wince of pain. "Have you been taking your pills?"

She refused to look at him, "Sometimes."

"Little Girl, you won't get better unless you take it regularly. If you don't take them every day, you'll not stop the pain."

"I do not want the pain to stop." The blue flashes spit out anger.

Pop was surprised, "Why on earth not?"

"If it stops hurting, then it makes my love for him not real. If it goes away, so does the memories. I do not want to forget what we had. I do not want to forget the sound of his voice, or...or...or the smile that made him irresistible, or the green twinkle of his eyes when he looked at me. I love him. It is real, and I will never forget. I do not want time to heal the wounds. I do not want him dead. I just want...it really does not matter what I want, does it. It is too late."

"Those are all perfectly normal feelings, but what would Nicholas think of you letting your health go that way over him? You still have his children to raise. They have had two dads stolen from them; they can't handle losing their mom on top of it. Listen, I spent my whole life regretting and mourning for the loss of Nicky. My wife blamed herself, my son blamed himself, and I blamed myself. We all let that blame consume our lives, and now my wife and son are dead because of it. We stopped trusting in God. We even blamed Him for it all, and all we got in return was years of grief, loneliness, and no relationship with our Maker. Whatever the reasons are, God had a good one for taking Nicky from all of us. I don't understand it, but he is gone. If you let yourself get sick, Sarah and Anna will be the ones to suffer. Is that what you want for my grandbabies?"

She hesitated. The edge seemed to fade from her tone, "It does not seem real. I cannot make myself lose this… this… this….in the bottom of my gut feeling, this knot that says it is not real. He is here, all around me. I feel a gnawing that I cannot shake."

"He *is* with you Park. He is in your heart. As long

as you and those two babies live, he will be real and living in your memories. You two shared something phenomenal that few people ever experience. It won't fade away that easily."

"It did with Matt?" Her voice trembled under her tears. "What he and I shared was an incredible young love, and he faded from my memories."

"But," comforted the father-in-law, "what you had with my son surpassed all understanding."

Park was still rubbing her hand over her chest. "I am so afraid that I will forget him. He was wonderful you know."

Pop walked with Park to the house to make sure she began her medicine. He began watching her more carefully and insisting on playing the part of her nurse. He would be for her what his son no longer could.

Pop was right. She valued her girls and determined to be a better mother. For the remainder of their visit, she joined them in hiking, boating, and fishing. At least she put on a good pretense of enjoyment. Her sweet girls need not suffer any more than necessary.

You Are Leaving Too.

Sarah held her sorrow under the cover of her responsibility for her mother. She was like Matt in this way, but she was like her mother in the fact that she was incredibly strong and resilient.

Anna reacted by having bad dreams. This was her way of dealing with what her young mind could not comprehend. She would be enrolling in kindergarten in the fall, and her daddy was not there to see her go. Anna was her daddy's girl, and he was no longer there. She took to sleeping with her mother, which seemed to comfort her sleeplessness.

The night before they flew home Pop, had another opportunity to have a heart-to-heart with the bereaved woman. She was more stable and somewhat stronger. The two watched the flames flickering from the relaxing fire, until they were both hardly holding their eyes open.

"Park," that was the first time he had used her

Christian name in over a year. Park took notice, "I don't know how you feel about me, but I am ready to tell you how I feel about you. Arrangements need to be made, and we might as well do it now as not."

She looked at him curiously, "Okay."

He began again, "You were my son's wife, but to me, you were the angel that returned my son to me. Had you never been married to him, I would never have come to know him."

"I really did not do anything," she protested.

"Don't talk, just listen. I love you. You are as dear to me as Kathy is. You are a daughter to me. Those two sleeping in there are my grandbabies. I would not want to separate from them, ever. If you cut them out of my life, you might as well cut out my heart. I do not want to impose on your good graces, and I am not sure how you feel, so I am going to buy a house in Charleston in order to be near my little girls. If that is too much assumption on my part, please tell me now."

"I should say it is!" she retorted. "Are you telling me you are not happy living with us?"

"No, I am very happy. I just don't want to intrude."

She knelt down at the old man's knees, with her hand on his, "I thank you for what you said. I have never had a father before. I am honored you think of me as a daughter, and I shall cherish you as a father, always. I love you, and so do Sarah and Anna. If you were not happy with us, I would understand. Be that as it may, your place is with us. You are family. Until you tire of us, this is a permanent invitation. We want you with us. I cannot believe you want to leave me too."

He patted her brown head, "Then it is settled. Tomorrow, we go *home*."

The memories of Nicholas did not hasten from the ones who loved him. Months passed by, and his presence was still just as real. Park did not hurry to get his things removed from the house. The remnants served as a balm for her, seemingly the only comfort she had.

Wearing his shirts comforted her. His toothbrush remained in the holder where it always had been. His pillow served as a console for her and Anna.

She wondered how long it would take her to stop thinking about him constantly. In order to expedite this result, she reported to work immediately and requested longer missions that would keep her mind occupied.

Fred watched her smile, but never saw the enchantment return to it. His Precious was broken, and he did not know how to fix her.

Nicholas's death had a tremendous ripple effect at work. The entire commission of coworkers mourned for their lost agent. His life affected the lives of many. Few spoke of him around his widow, though.

Richardson reluctantly gave Park the longer assignments she wanted, pulling her from a few that were near suicide missions. He feared she would willingly die for the service of her country if given half a chance.

Bruce and Christy saw little of their friend. Pop kept the girls more and more, and Sonya was not getting to hang around her best friend as much. A pall rested upon these friends.

Park seemed more distant to her old friend. No matter what Bruce tried, he could not gap that distance. Christy helped him realize one day that his best friend had, somewhere along the way, found another best friend in her husband.

The Beginning of Friendship

Bruce Clayton, nicknamed 'Squeaky', because of his squeaky clean appearance, was ten years old when he met little Mary Ann Livingston. As an initiation into a gang or ne'er-do-wells, he was to trick this girl into their lair in order to scare her. They were not planning to hurt her; they just wanted to see her cry in order to get their boyish thrills.

The group of boys awaited their prey. Squeaky lured the girl in by pretending to be her friend where the boys circled the unsuspecting kid, taunting her with words.

In reaction, she tightened her jaw and faced each one of them, which infuriated the band of boys. When she refused them the pleasure of being scared, the first one struck her across the face, but she did not flinch. This infuriated them more. Two more circled around and landed a fist in her stomach. She moved only to accommodate the blows. She steadily looked her persecutors in the eye, determinedly.

47

Bruce was ready to get out of there. They were not supposed to touch her. He did not want any part of this. He was ready to flee, when it came to his facing her eyes. Probing blue searched the brown eyes that had betrayed her.

The boys were still punching. Her lip bled real blood. This was not a joke any more. "Stop it!" he shouted, but they paid him no heed. He ran to the middle of the circle, grabbed her arm and yanked hard which relieved the cowards of their grip. He held her hand and ran until they were out of danger.

When he removed his shirt to replace hers that had been torn, he became aware of the violent scars on her back. Quickly, he covered her bare skin and continued the journey.

He took her to his mother and explained what had happened. His mother had been so disappointed in him. He felt worse when she spoke not a word of rebuke. She cleaned the little girl up and put her in a warm bed. Bruce told his mother that she lived in the orphanage, so she could call and let them know she was safe.

He never forgot how disappointed his mother had been. His dear sweet mother never scolded him, because she knew he learned his lesson the hard way.

From that point on, the two friends were inseparable. Mary Ann readily forgave him his deeds. She explained about a Christ who suffered much, died on a rugged cross, and rose from the grave to forgive her of her wickedness. Soon after, He became Bruce's Lord.

He owed his life to that little girl. Those blue eyes of hers saved him from a life of crime.

How was he going to restore himself to his rightful place in Park's heart as best friend? How was he going to save her from the depression that overtook her? How could he reinstate Jesus as the Lord and Master of her life, when she was so angry with Him?

Ailing Anna

She performed her duties mechanically, rarely attending the home church she loved so much. So many wanted to help this beloved one. However, none knew how, because she leaned not unto the Lord. Nevertheless, God saw one of His had fallen and was not responding, so in His infinite wisdom, to draw her to her knees once more, He inflicted Anna.

Park was in the middle of a long assignment when Richardson pulled her out. Not knowing how to get her at work, Pop had called Bruce, who called Fred, who relayed the message to Richardson that Pop had taken little Anna to the hospital. They were not sure what the problem was, but she was exhausted all the time, and could not stay awake. Her temperature fluctuated between 101.3° and 102.7°.

Anna had not wakened for a full day now. Bruce and Christy were at her side; after all, this was their little one too. Reinforcements were established. The prayer band was set; all except a mother, who was still angry with the One to whom they prayed.

Park lay beside her baby, holding her in her bosom. Even now, tears refused to surface. In fact, worry lines appeared on the beautiful face. Two days passed and still the mother did not turn to God.

It was Bruce who broached the subject when he came in the third morning. "How is she doing this morning?"

"The same." She replied in the same blunt and emotionless way as of late.

"Have the doctors been in this morning?"

"Not yet."

Her short answers were not helping him prepare for the difficult conversation ahead. "Have they determined what is wrong with her yet?" She shook her head. "Well, no matter. We know God is the only One that can heal our little girl."

"Yes He is, but is He willing?" Bruce was astonished at the bitterness he heard. This could not be that little girl that forgave him so long ago.

"What makes you think He is not willing, Sweetie?"

"Because she loves me."

"And that warrants what exactly?" he pressed.

"Oh Bruce, you can see the handwriting on the wall just like I can. Every time someone loves me, He takes them. Matt, Nick, our baby, and now Anna. I only have one more to give."

"I love you Park, and I am still here. He has not taken me. How do you account for that in your grand plan?"

"Give Him time. Don't wish it upon yourself."

"Honey, He loves us." She scoffed, but he continued, "You know He does, and sometimes He gives us trials in which He tries to let us find out how we will react in them.

He already knows how we will do, but we need to know. How strong are you in the faith? Are you going to disappoint Him on the last mile? If we never have trials, then we never realize His mercy. It is pretty easy to live on the mountain tops, but it is how we handle the valleys that count."

"Bruce, I am tired of the trials. I don't have the strength to fight anymore. Will there never be an end to them?"

"Probably not, but that is why He said, '*Come unto Me, all ye that labor and are heavy laden, and I will give you rest. Take My yoke upon you, and learn of me; for I am meek and lowly in heart: and ye shall find rest unto your souls.*' When did you stop resting in Him, Friend? You were reliant on Him for your very breath, and now, when will you come unto Him again?"

"I did not stop resting in Him. He left me."

"Park O'Ryan, you know that is not true one bit!"

"Yes, it is. And Anna, what did she do to deserve this?"

"As I live and breathe, I do not know this woman before me today. You have changed and not for the better, either."

"I don't care any more."

Prayers of a Saint

Stumped as to how to continue, her friend waited a few minutes. "Remember the day we met and Mom took you in for the night? I told her what I did to you. She never said a cross word to me about it. It was worse than any punishment she could have dealt. It ate at me.

I told her how amazing I thought you were to be so tough. I asked Mom how you could be my friend after I played a dirty trick on you like that. I will never forget what she said to me. She was talking about the scars on your back. 'Son,' she told me, 'those are battle wounds. She has been in a war with the devil. He may have tried his best and left his marks, but she gave the battle to God. When the Lord fights your battles, He never loses. God said in I John 4:4, *Ye are of God, little children, and have overcome them: because greater is He that is in you, than he that is in the world.*' I told Mom how I wanted to be fearless like you, and she told me what I had to do to be saved. Do you remember the conditions Park, in which you must be saved?"

"I was too stupid to be scared," she averted.

"He said you had to have child-like faith. My friend, what happened to that child in you that I treasured? Will you please send her home, because her old friend, Bruce, really misses her a lot?"

"I am too tired. I have neither strength nor desire to fight anymore."

"Just lean on Him and let Him do it for you. Come," he knelt beside the sick bed, waiting for his friend to do the same. He held her hand and gently guided her to her knees. "*Our* Heavenly Father, we bow before the throne of grace once more in humility. We come before Your presence with thanksgiving, to ask You to advocate to the Father. Your child needs your mercy and guidance. I ask You please to bring her back to the fold. She is in desperate need of healing. We know this is one of the times You carry her. We ask also for the little girl in the sick bed that You would put Your healing touch on her tiny body, according to Thy will. Forgive us of our sins, we pray."

For the first time in all these months, tears flowed from the hardened soul. Here she was, with her innocent little baby at death's door, and all she could do is feel sorry for herself. Her own selfishness sickened her. She had no right to ask God for anything. Putting her pride away, she prayed for Anna's sake.

"Oh God, I am so ashamed. I have failed this trial miserably. I beg You for forgiveness, please. Please cover me in that atoning blood once more. I am so unworthy of any blessings that you have already given me. How dare I ask for more? You brought me out of a living hell and placed me on the solid Rock. For that, I shall thank You forever. May I ask You please...please help my Anna? I know that it is in Your hands, and no one can save her but You. Please, oh God, not for my sake, but for Matt's and for Nick's, will You make her whole?" Suddenly, the dam burst, "Will you take care of my two guys until I come Home? Will You lead and guide me and help me to wait upon You, and not get ahead of Your will? I need You more now than I ever did before. If I may find mercy in Thy sight, please, Father. I come to You in the precious name of Jesus, not my will, but Thy will be done. Amen."

Anna was peeping over the side of her hospital bed, "Momma, you came home."

Tears and laughter crowded the words away, so the two scooped the little one up, hugged, and kissed her abundantly. Anna was not aware that she had been sleeping for almost three days. She was just glad that her mommy was here. Everything was always better when mommy was home.

Shawn Grayson

After spending five months mourning for her lover, Park realized it was the appropriate time to be comforted in the Savior's arms. What peace filled her soul! She had failed the test, but God would always forgive her and try her again.

It was time that Park O'Ryan began the new life of being single parent to her children. She compromised with Richardson to work only when he absolutely needed her. She also took Kincaid up on his offer to teach new recruits how to fly the military aircraft, which would place her at home every night. This would only last about twelve weeks at a time, twice a year.

Between Matt and her, and Nick and her, they had saved enough money to get them through any hard times, so they would not have to worry about finances. She would just wait on the Lord to show her what to do next.

Bruce was pleased that he had his best friend back

and closer, now she was working at the base. Christy watched her husband taking care of his old friend with admiration and pride.

Fred frequented the Air Force base for lunch with Precious. He missed not having her around the work place all the time. When the annual gala event for the POWs rolled around, he was overjoyed that Park asked him to be her escort.

She made it simple this year, omitting the girls to come along. She would just show up out of politeness and leave as soon as possible.

Fred arrived on her step sporting a tuxedo, which Park had never seen before. He looked so debonair and distinguished. She teased him about how handsome he looked, saying that if only he were a few years younger or she a few years older, she would feel honored to court such a handsome man.

The conference room filled with black coats and shiny dresses. Among the sea of black sparkle, Shawn approached her and Fred curiously. "You must be Park's father." He reached his hand to Fred.

"Fred's the name," returning the handshake and smile.

"Shawn Grayson. Pleasure to meet you." He turned to Park, "You are as lovely as always, Park. Where is that husband of yours?"

Fred froze. He had not anticipated someone asking about Nick, but Park smiled her charm, "Nicholas was killed a few months ago, Shawn. Where is your mother tonight?"

"I am sorry to hear that. Mom is over here. Come on, she will want to see you." He led the couple through the maze of mingling guests, "Mother, look who I found."

The delicate older woman hugged the one who had brought her long lost son home to her. "My dear, it is so good to see you. I cannot believe it has been another year already."

"Mrs. Grayson, I would like you to meet my beloved friend, Fred. Fred, this is Shawn's mother."

"Please dear, call me Martha. It is a pleasure to meet you, Fred."

The elegant gentleman beside her lifted the delicate lady hands to his lips. "Pleasure is all mine."

"Would you get me a drink, Fred?" Martha said in her own charming way. The two walked off arm in arm.

After the dinner, Shawn presented a short speech. Park was ready to go home. She offered her excuses to Shawn, but he asked her to stay. He would take her home if Fred did not object. To Park's annoyance, Fred was pleased to escort Mrs. Grayson home.

It was late when Shawn drove her home. She did not feel it was appropriate to just send him home, yet she was not comfortable asking him inside, either. She compromised by inviting him for a walk on the beach. It was a cold December night. The stars sparkled overhead in the clear sky proclaiming the season of Christmas.

They walked a way before either spoke, "I am sorry to her about Nicholas. He was a good man. It is a shame he is gone."

"The Lord has His reasons. It is not ours to ask why, but I do thank you. It has been lonely without him."

"Has anyone ever told you how incredible you are? I mean it. You have a passion about you that few people have. Take this POW cause, for example. Some people who have experienced war do not feel as strongly and compassionately as you do about it. It does not seem fitting that a young one like you should fret over us old timers. Your generation just seemed to forget about wars or their veterans. That makes you a rare breed." She made no response, he continued. "Dad knew there was something special about you and I agree."

"Why did you never marry, Shawn? How come you did not have a wife at home, pining away for your return from war?" They turned to walk back toward the house.

"I almost did have one before I went off. Sarah Jane Parker would make my heart stop, but she ran off with Billy Watkins, who couldn't go to war because of high blood pressure. I never saw her again. It seems that the women nowadays are flaky and irresponsible. They only care if their nails get broken. You are one in a million. No, I probably will never get to the altar."

She softly smiled. "Well, here we are. It is rather late. Will I see you again sometime?"

"I hope so. May I call on you, soon? I would like to discuss something with you I think you would be interested in."

"Sure. Goodnight, Mr. Grayson."

"It is Shawn. Goodnight to you, too."

Richardson's Surprise

Winter spread her white over the mountains, and on occasion would prevent the O'Ryans and Pop from attending church. Even Pop had a renewed faith in the Holy Spirit, since the family attended regularly.

In obeisance to waiting on an answer from above, Park spent days riding Spirit to the field that she used to take Nicholas. She did not want to chance losing her Peace again. Waiting for His divine intervention, she patiently basked in the victory Jesus had claimed for her. Having repented of the sin of hatred and being fully cleansed under the Blood of Jesus, she was able to hear from the Father once more.

Richardson called her in one Tuesday, asking her to come by headquarters at the end of class to discuss something important. She tried to put him off, but he persisted.

"Gorshev is alive! How?" her boss demanded. "I

thought you killed him."

She defended in astonishment, "I filled him with bullets, sir. I felt his pulse, there was none."

"Are you absolutely positive he was dead, O'Ryan?"

"Beyond a shadow of a doubt, sir."

"Then we have a problem."

She puzzled, "I do not understand."

Either the man you thought you killed was not the real Gorshev, or he has an identical twin." He turned to the intercom, "Zoë, have you found anything yet?"

"No sir. The search is almost complete," Zoë responded.

"Bring it in as soon as you get it." He flipped the button. "If there is a brother, we may have a link to a bombing in Brussels last month, one in Pakistan in October, and the bombing in Marseilles four days ago. It would explain the Marseilles bombing was for revenge on

Enrique, who died in that bombing. There are at least five known survivors of the Kiev incident from his movement. How they escaped, I do not know. We caught one of them, but he popped cyanide before we could extract any information."

"Where did you catch him?"

"Mullins saw him in an art museum during the Lativia assignment. He recognized him from your Kiev mission."

"Sir," Zoë entered, "I have it. The DNA from the sight proved that Gorshev was the man Park killed. Back in 1957, there *was* a set of twins born to the Gorshevs. The government would not allow them to keep both, so they faked the birth certificate, and left the other on the steps of an orphanage. Years later, the underworld grapevine has it that the two reunited underground and started this league called Rebel Righters. I have traced the Marseilles bombing to the Rebel Righters. So far I haven't gotten anything back on the other two bombings, but I bet it will be the same."

"When do we leave?" said Park, forgetting her other responsibilities.

"*We* don't. You're not going," commanded Richardson.

Zoë agreed, "He's right, Park, you are targeted. You are the one that pulled the trigger that killed his brother. You have a price on your head. You can't go."

"That is all the more reason I should go. If they are hunting me, it will be easier for me to find them." No sooner were the words out of her mouth that the Spirit moved on her. Not wanting to grieve the Holy Spirit, Park recanted her statement. It was not His will, so she would not go.

Richardson concluded, "Go home; act normal, and we will call you when we know something."

"Yes sir."

"And Park…"

"Yes?" She turned to leave.

"Watch your back. There's a hefty price on your head. They won't hesitate to kill anyone around you."

Afterlife

Six weeks passed while Park patiently waited for the call. She spent many of these hours on her knees in prayer. Her body wanted her to go fight the man that was partially responsible for Nicholas's death, but her Guide refused her permission. She waited for Him to reveal His will to her.

When her phone rang and her code name called, she made haste to the headquarters.

"We destroyed the Gorshev compound," Richardson explained. "It was another chemical factory. It is obvious they were concentrating on taking you out. He had possession of some serious information. They even had a target on your friends."

"It appears as if God is watching over me." She smiled to her Father with a silent, "Thank You."

Richardson added, "It is better than we could hope for. It is the location where they have been holding the captured agents. We have retrieved all agents from their clutches." His pause made Park nervous. "They have done unspeakable things to these men and women." He turned toward the window. "Park, we found Nicholas."

Her heart jumped. "Nick is alive? Where is he? I want to see him."

Richardson held his hand up for her to stop, "Not so fast. I said we found him. Park, he is not the same man that left here."

"What do you mean?"

"They injected him with a drug that messed with his brain. He does not even know who he is."

"Where is he?"

"He is in med four." As Park turned to leave, he threw at her, "Park, be prepared."

Park flew to the medical room four. She could see him through the door. He was there in the flesh. His strong back was weaker and his hair was long and disheveled. She started when he turned his wild green eyes in her direction like a caged animal.

It motivated her to push through the door. He lunged at her to escape, taking her unaware. She literally fought him off. He screamed the ranting of a lunatic.

Park worked her way back out. She stood with the locked door between her and the man she loved. He did not know her at all. "Please give me strength, dear God. For all I have in me, please help me through this. Please help Nicholas. You are his only Help," she breathed to herself audibly.

Richardson was behind her. "I hope God can help him."

"He is the only One who can. Nicholas will recover according to His will."

"You left before I finished debriefing you. You need to know that Gorshev escaped. He went so far underground we cannot find him. With the information, we found at the compound, you are in real danger. You might want to relocate everyone until this is cleared up."

"Begging your pardon sir, but my children should not have to uproot and look over their shoulder because of me. If Gorshev wants me then I will make it easy for him to get *me*."

"As long as you understand the situation. We can discuss this later. I am meeting with Doctor Martin in ten minutes to get the results of Nicholas's tests. Come, we'll go together."

The doctor placated, "Park, it is good to see you again. The tests revealed that they injected Nicholas with a drug that they concocted. There has been virtually no testing on this drug. It is still in its infancy, and we do not know the long-term effects of it. What we do know is that Nick has suffered irreparable damage to a percentage of cells in the frontal lobe. We can go in surgically and repair what we can. As far as the memories he has lost, we will have to wait and see. Chances are, Park, what he has already lost will never come back. This is not an emotional blockage of choice but a physical destruction. With this procedure, we are hoping to stabilize the part that has disoriented him. It is our only chance."

Park continued in prayer. "What alternative do we have? He has no memory either way. We cannot let him continue as if he were an animal."

"It is unanimous then. Start right away." Having said that, Richardson left.

"We will begin in a couple of hours. You can watch from the observatory if you like. Where will you be, so I can call you when it is time?" asked the doctor.

"I will wait in the observatory."

Park spent those two hours alone in prayer. She could not fathom what kind of human could fill her sweet, kind Nicholas's mind with madness. She had lost Nick's love, but God had restored his life. She was thankful for that.

She was undeserving of his love and lost it. She comprehended her responsibility in the horror. Her disobedience to God and killing for hatred caused her this agony. If she had not killed Gorshev, she could have forced him to tell the truth. Nicholas would not have suffered this tragedy. Her rebellion against God would cause all those whom she loved to suffer a lifetime. Although He already had, she pleaded with God to forgive her again.

She had a second chance with Nicholas. God had been merciful to her.

Going Home

Fred came by after duty and stayed with her for the remainder of the surgery. His quiet presence helped ease the tension. In showing his love for her husband, he showed his love for her.

The exhausted doctor completed the procedure. Now, came the waiting. Park stayed by her husband's side, praying and watching for almost a week. He had suffered an injury to the skull and healing would take time.

At last, he rewarded her by opening his eyes and looking around. He no longer ranted wildly. He did not speak at all. He just closed the green pools and went to sleep. Park did not see the ferociousness in them this time.

He woke a few times that night to find a brown mass resting at his side. Tired, weary, and ignorant, he drifted into a deep sleep each time.

Park spoke sweet words to the former lover every day. She got her Bible and read his old favorite passages, which seemed to soothe his pain.

Dr. Martin confirmed that the loss of memories was permanent, but the procedure was successful otherwise. In a few days, they would get him up and he would be like new in no time at all as far as the physical aspect of it went.

Richardson checked in daily for a progress report on Nicholas O'Ryan's healing shell. It might take years, but it was worth it to replace that Park's life back in one piece. Anything that Nicholas should need he would make sure he had.

The removal of bandages revealed short dark stubble, where the doctor shaved his head for surgery. Every day Park placed her hands on his short fuzz and prayed for God to show her His will.

The strange Nicholas came to know the nurse that stayed with him always. Others would come in, but he would cling to her. She was agreeable and pleasant. She seemed to take a special interest in him.

She had told no one of his existence yet. At the beginning, she feared the surgery might fail and there would be no point in putting the girls and Pop through another mourning. The fact that she had not spoken to anyone because she had not left his side made that decision easier.

Finally, the day came when she could take him home. Park called Pop and asked him to meet her at the house without the girls, because she had something very important to show him.

The old man was sitting on the deck nervously waiting to see what his little girl needed that was so important. That Grayson fellow had been coming around some. He hoped he was not getting wedding news.

Park explained to Nicholas that he was going home. Though she had not told him he was her husband, he followed her without question. She was not sure how much he could comprehend if she did tell him much.

Nicholas observed all the surroundings as Park drove to the house. He made several exclamations and asked many questions. Park had to side step many of his questions.

Revival

Park led Nicholas through the kitchen door where Albert McCrain froze. There were tears in his old eyes. "Park?"

"Nicholas, this is your dad, Albert McCrain."

The confused old man stammered, "But, but, but..."

"Pop, it is truly him. They found him alive, but he has no recollection at all. He has permanent loss of memory, but God is good to bring him back to us."

"But...but...but..."

Nicholas spoke in slow rehearsed words, "You are my father?" He understood the concept of a father but had no memory of this man.

"My son!" Pop embraced his son for a long time. Park discreetly left the two alone. "My boy, we thought you were dead. My boy! It is so good to hold you again.

Did they hurt you?"

"I do not remember. They told me that some bad people held me for eight months in a bad place, where they did something to my mind."

"My son!" was all the father could utter.

"Is this where I live? Park said I was going home."

"Yes, you and Park lived here."

"She was my nurse? Why did I need a nurse?"

The age had fallen from the man, "Son, Park is your wife. You have two beautiful children, and we all five live here."

"She's my wife?" he puzzled. "I have children? No one told me of these things." All this news overwhelmed the invalid.

"Sarah and Anna. My son, it is so wonderful to have you home."

The revelations had taken their toll on the foundling. "I'm feeling tired." He did not know how everyone expected him to act.

"Of course you are. There is plenty of time later to talk about all this." The father called, "Park! Nicholas is getting tired."

Park rushed back down, having removed all her belongings from their room. "Nicholas, I will show you to your room." She led him to the second story bedroom. "I will be right downstairs, if you need me. Your clothes are in the drawers and closet, if you would like to change into something more comfortable. You get some rest."

She went to pull down the shades. "How long have we been married?" he asked.

Park startled briefly, "A year and a half before you were... before your...accident."

"Oh."

"Would you like something to drink?"

82

"No, thank you. Where are my children?"

Again, he surprised her, "They are staying at a friend's house. I have not told them you were home yet."

"This is all so new to me. I try and try, but I cannot remember anything."

"Do not try, Nicholas. You cannot remember. They removed that part of your memory. You will overexert yourself trying to remember what you cannot. Now rest a while."

Park called Bruce to meet her at the house. She wanted to have to explain the details only one time. She sat down with Pop and Bruce and explained every detail. The explanation exposed their being secret agents for the US government.

Pop was astonished. The two listened to the details of the fateful assignment and the revelation that Gorshev had lied about Nicholas dying. She explained what the fiends had done to his mind. It was hard to convey the fact that he would *never* remember his past. They could try hard as they might, but that part of his life was gone permanently.

The Healing Cabin

Spring break was coming up, and Park wanted to take Nicholas to their healing ground. He needed to revive the primitive basic instincts. Pop said he would drive the trip with the girls, so he could stop in Kansas in person to tell Kathy. Park would fly Nicholas on up ahead, giving them time to work on reeducating him about his personal life.

She had to clear it through Richardson first. Debriefing on this level would take extra time, He agreed to the trip under the condition that Nicholas was to report to the headquarters upon their return.

Nicholas was glad for the time alone. He did not know this woman who claimed to be his wife, so he was glad when she gave him space. He became nervous about the Montana trip, especially the part about two days alone with this person. Everybody was foreign to him, even his father. Why could he not remember his own father?

Reading his fears, Park set up camp in the old tractor shed for her sleeping arrangements, leaving Nicholas to himself. She would cook and clean for him and take him in the boat. She kept close enough to help him if need be, yet far enough to let him feel free enough to explore his situation.

He did not feel right about her sleeping outside, while he lay in a warm bed. There was another bedroom in the house, yet she insisted on the shed.

On the way up, Park ordered the materials to build a tree house for Sarah and Anna. This would prove a productive way to pass the time. The materials arrived the second day, and they began building.

Nicholas spent some good quality alone time on the lake or walking in the woods. He tried hard to remember anything, but couldn't. He tried to think of ways to trigger these memories back in place, but only received a headache for his efforts until Park would rescue him.

On one of these rescues, she found him sitting on a

log resting quietly on a bed of pine needles. He lay back on the log, deep in thought and did not hear Park approach him. When he realized her presence, he startled and fell off the log, which knocked Park to the ground. The melody of her laugh warmed his heart. She was a pleasant person after all.

After climbing back on the log, she searched his scalp to make sure no injuries had incurred from the fall. He lifted his green eyes that held no acknowledgement of her. What she would give to have Nicholas back!

In an attempt to jolt a memory, he stole a kiss from his wife. She briefly allowed it, but then quickly pulled away and retreated, when she realized he did not feel a thing. There was no memory in that kiss. He would have to accept that he would never have that advantage again.

Park wanted nothing more at that moment, than to fall into her husband's arms, but the coldness in that kiss reminded her that she was foreign to him.

Who Am I?

That evening, after Park washed all the dishes and headed to the door, Nicholas had thousands of questions to ask and pleaded with her to stay. "Do you have to go now?" his voice was the same as Nicholas, yet the soul was that of an unknown.

She responded, "Is there anything wrong?"

"I would like to talk. That is, if you don't mind."

Park shut the open door and retreated to the floor in front of the fireplace. Nicholas carefully perched himself on the arm of the couch.

"What kind of person was I?"

An endearing smile enveloped her, radiating the beauty in her heart. Her demeanor became soft and angelic. Park realized that she may be a stranger to him, but he was a stranger to himself.

She spoke adoringly, "You were a wonderfully incredible man. You were strong and sure. Your faith interceded Heaven for my sake many times, because you walked so close to God. You were kind, gentle, and so very, very loving. You charmed me into loving you before I knew what to do and fell hopelessly in love with you."

His next question was, "How did we meet each other?"

"You transferred to my division as the best agent from your division, and Richardson teamed you with me."

"Was it love at first sight?"

She smiled a sadly charming smile, "You told me for you it was. You said the first time you ever laid eyes on me you knew there would never be another for you."

"You did not feel the same way?" There was a tender offense in his question.

"I was in love with my husband." Nick looked at her

surprised. Quickly, she explained, "Matt and I were childhood sweethearts. He had been my whole life, until he was killed."

"Was he like us? Did he work for Richardson?"

"No, he was a Colonel in the Air Force. He liked you a lot. You used to come to our cookouts. You met Fred. You, he, and Jenny, your temporary partner while I was pregnant with Anna, shared a lot of fun at our house."

He looked confused. "Albert told me Anna was my daughter. You mean you were married to this Matt when we..."

"Oh, no!" she recovered, "Matt is Sarah and Anna's biological father. When you and I married, you adopted them as your own."

He stood up, "I am thirsty. Would you like something to drink?" Park jumped to her feet to serve him, but he objected, "I can get it. You cannot continue to treat me like a baby. Would you like something?"

"No, thank you."

Nicholas stood in the doorway upon his return, and watched this stranger-wife. She had relieved the falling pins from her hair and sat hugging her knees, while the flames danced in her hair. Her loveliness touched his heart with sadness.

"This is a nice place." He joined her in front of the hearth, placing a cushion from the sofa behind her.

She enlightened, "This is your place. You introduced me to this haven of rest in my time of need. Anna was born here. You rescued me."

"Were you still married, then?"

"That is why I was here. Matt died days before Anna was born, and I was in a bad emotional state. I came here to find Peace. Later, I found you."

"Was I ever mean to anybody? I couldn't have been this superman you have portrayed."

"You were every bit of a superman and more. You were decent, caring, and wonderful. There seems to be no words that can sufficiently describe you. You were unique."

He continued to pommel her with questions for hours. She wearied herself in giving the best answers she could to give him back the character that had made him so fine. She displayed her admiration in the person he used to be.

Somewhere in between pauses in topics, the fair-haired maiden fell into the slumbers of the night, resting her mass of brown locks on the cushion.

Nicholas scrutinized her features as she slept. Her youthful face hid lines of worry or distress. Subtle as they were, they faintly painted her as a more sophisticated character.

He dared touch her small hand that bore calluses from hard work. It was void of painted nails. Instead, they were clean and pink. He noticed a scar below the knuckles, and in turning her hand over, a larger scar tried to hide.

Her lips curved invitingly in relaxation, and her breast rose and fell under the deep breaths of slumber. The vision filled him with a longing that his new childish mind could not understand. He watched her in awe, stricken with paralysis for hours.

The next morning brought the remaining troops from home. Anna would not leave her Daddy's side. The whole week she shadowed his every move, but Sara clung to grandpa.

She held aloof of her new dad. He did not look at Momma the way he used to, and he did not act as if he loved them at all. Her mind could not understand that he had no memory of them.

Pop retold many stories to fill in the missing pieces to his son's life, giving him a piece of the past the horrible men stole from him, until the days were gone. It was time to head home.

Anna pleaded with her mom to let her stay and fly home with them the next day. She climbed in Nicholas's lap and showered him with kisses, until her mother complied.

Grandpa and Sarah left the day before the fliers took off, leaving Anna with Mom and Dad alone, at last. She had her Daddy back, and she was ready to make up for lost time. She made him take her fishing in the boat.

While they fished, Park hiked into the mountain. This was her haven of rest, and she fully intended to use it as such. The clean air filled her with its cleansing power. She successfully fought the flood of memories that threatened to deluge her healing.

This was God in His awesomeness.

Absence Makes The Heart Grow Fonder

Park suffered through bronchitis because of her early summer camping trip in Montana and had missed some work. She took this time to be still and wait to hear from her Lord what to do about her husband.

Nicholas's body had healed. He had learned about his personal life, now he wanted to learn how to be a man and support his family again.

He checked in with Richardson as scheduled and began an extensive eighteen-week training. His academic skills had not much been affected. Nonetheless, it would take a lot of work.

Park continued with a few assignments and did not see Nicholas for the duration of his training. He lived at the headquarters and saw little of the outside world as was typical procedure for new recruits.

The girls wondered when Daddy was coming home during his months of training. They missed him and felt their mother had taken him from them again. Sarah began growing resentful of her mother.

He was eager to learn and trained hard. A lot of his natural ability resurfaced. The doctor informed Richardson that in another year, he should resume to agent status.

Once he was out of immediate training, Fred sought him out to renew their friendship. He shared stories that he thought were appropriate to reveal. A few things he thought best to keep to himself.

Nicholas began to think about that woman he had not seen in a while. He remembered her soft lips as he kissed her that day. He remembered that adoring look when she told him stories around the fire. His heart started warming to these memories.

The first time he saw her after intense training was in Richardson's office in prep for an assignment. He did not get to speak to her because she was in with the big guy.

He was not aware that Park was keeping a close eye on him. She was not about to lose sight of him again.

In completion of his in-house training, Richardson assigned Nicholas his first assignment with Park as team leader, knowing she would pull the best results from him.

It was a simple one-day job. The instinct Nicholas had with firing weapons and combat seemed to remain in the old shell.

He watched his stranger-wife in action, admiring her agility and grace. That sweet angel he had come to know in Montana put on a sober face, responded with a determination, and awed him with her ability.

The October winds blew in a hurricane that rendered Charleston torn. It destroyed houses and blew away businesses, but that brick house on the ocean, stood firm, waiting the arrival of its former master.

Finally, Richardson released Nicholas from training.

He was finally going home. He was half-anxious to have the opportunity to find out what spell this woman had over him, which would not let him forget that kiss or her sleeping form in front of the fire.

However, he was still to put this exploration of emotions on hold because the one whom he awaited requested a long assignment. In compliance, Richardson sent her on a three-week job in Afghanistan.

Bruce did not make himself a stranger to the old-new friend. He wanted to help replace all that he could, so he sat for hours reminiscing over pictures, gifts, and old stories during Park's absence.

Nicholas listened as Bruce described her and wondered about their relationship. This man sounded as if he cherished her. Bruce told him how heartbroken Park was when she thought he was dead. The man had fires burning within by the time Bruce finished. If he did not love her before, Bruce's ability to describe her changed that.

Then there was Pop, who hinted and pushed until Nicholas really thought he felt something for this girl. If everyone was for it, maybe he should not be against it.

Only Sarah seemed against the reunion of husband and wife. The new father took objection to her wanting to spend so much time at Sonya's house, feeling she did not like her dad very much. She made pleas every night to spend the night away.

Temper Tantrum

Nicholas became bolder throughout his training. His personal attitude had matured. He tolerated and excused Sarah's avoidance for a while, but then one night, he chose to stand his ground and asked her to stay home.

"I want you to stay home tonight, Honey. You're gone every night."

"Why?" she spouted. "You don't want me here."

Nicholas was astonished at her brazen reaction, "That is not true, Sarah. Of course, I want you here."

Seeing it hurt him, she snapped angrily, "No you don't. That's why Momma's not here. You don't want her around."

"Sarah, that's enough," rebuked her grandfather.

"It is true. He doesn't love us. He doesn't want us around at all, and I hate him!"

"Sarah, I *do* love you," argued the memory-free father.

"No you don't. You don't care at all. You don't care that when you left us Anna started having nightmares, and that Momma's bad dreams came back. You promised me you would always be there to comfort her, but you lied. You don't care that Momma's heart broke in half until she had to take pills, when you left. You don't care at all. You don't look at Momma the same way anymore, and you don't act like you even like us."

"Sarah O'Ryan!" commanded Grandpa. "What would your Momma say if she heard you speak like that?"

"She'd whip me, Grandpa," tears fought to surface.

"And she would have every right to. Now, go to your room." The reality of her actions came upon her as she sullenly left the room. Turning to Nicholas, Albert comforted, "Son, you can't let that bother you. She is a child and doesn't understand. She is angry, but she loves you."

"She said she hates me Dad. She is right. I have not been here for her. I do not know what promises I made before that I cannot keep. I do not blame her for hating me."

"Son, she does not hate you. If she didn't love you so much, she wouldn't be that angry."

"I have not been much of a father, or husband for that matter. I need to remember. I just can't, no matter how hard I try." He became frustrated.

The weary strange father determined to ask anyone he encountered about who he was and about his family. He had to learn somehow. They spent the week in Montana learning about him, and he had not asked anything about her.

To add aggravation, he hit a brick wall when he tried to learn information about her. Grandpa and Christy only knew her for the last few years, and Fred and Bruce would change the subject completely. They would speak of her character and position, but nothing in the way of personal history. These two dear friends of hers knew she would not like this information revealed. Pity was not in her forte.

"Curse her secrets!" he angrily concluded.

Running From Love

When Park returned from her assignment, she stopped at the stables and rode Spirit to the house. She devised a plan to avoid alone time with Nicholas.

Upon seeing the wraith-like vision floating down the beach on a prancing stallion, Nicholas's heart grew warm. Finally, he could get to know her.

"She is a beauty, isn't she," Pop said when he saw his son watching her approach.

"I wish I could remember what it was like. So many people tell me, but it is not the same."

"Make new memories, Son. You had the real thing with her once. Not everyone gets a second chance."

Nicholas shook his head, "I have been thinking. Maybe you are right, but I make no promises. I do want to come to know her better. I feel like a burden to her

104

now, some obligation she would never neglect."

"Hi, Pop!" she said brightly as she dismounted. "Nicholas, you are looking well. It is good to see you. Pop, where are my girls?"

"Sarah is over at Sonya's, and Anna is inside." He made a hasty exit so his two kids could talk.

"Are you trying to avoid me?" Nicholas asked bluntly.

"I'm sorry, what do you mean?" She could feel him searching her soul.

"Since I have been home, this is the first time I have seen you. Are you deliberately staying away?"

"I have been on assignment. That is my job, Nicholas. I am gone a lot. I am here now. Is something wrong? Are the girls okay?" she skirted.

Again, he retorted bluntly, "The girls miss you when you are gone. Anna cries every night for you."

"You are the one she wants comfort from. You are the one she misses. You are the only father she ever knew. She was your little girl, and she loves her Dad."

"What about you? Do you still love her Dad?"

"What I feel does not matter."

"Why not?" he asked.

Park was feeling uncomfortable and vulnerable now. "Let's concentrate on you and your needs for now. Have you found everything you need?"

"I need nothing." He knew she was trying to distract his attention away from her.

"Good. Now, I will go see my baby girl." Before he could protest, she was gone.

Pop approached when he saw Park pass. "How'd it go?"

"Dad, she has put the girls and me up front and will not deal with her own feelings of comfort."

"That's Park for you. You used to say she was the most stubborn woman you had ever met.

"I can see why," he grimaced.

Park returned shortly with a duffel bag in tow. "I thought about taking a short cruise on *Freedom's Park*, maybe a day or two."

"I think that would be nice, I will go get my bags. Dad, will you help Park get the girls' stuff together?" Nicholas was not about to relinquish her yet.

Park wanted to go alone, so she would not have to make him uncomfortable in his own home. She was trying to avoid having him feel things he was not ready to feel, but since he insisted on coming along, what could she do? She could not very well refuse him.

To her relief, before the yacht set sail, her phone rang. Nicholas and she had been ordered to report to work, which saved her of a night of awkwardness.

Captiv - ated

The assignment took them to Belgrade, where they had found a chemical plant that needed shutting down.

They rowed in by way of a canal to the targeted place. Upon arrival, there was no sign of living beings. The eight-man team searched in vain.

"Park and O'Ryan, stay back and get samples of everything. The rest of the team egress. Remember Park, a separate vial for each chemical. You do not know what will happen if you mix any of them," Richardson ordered into their communications device.

"It does not look like anyone has been here in a while, sir. There are cobwebs, which indicate several days. This must be a decoy. I am checking it out," Park responded.

"There is something in this other room, do you want me to get samples there?" asked Nicholas.

"Yes, I am going into that computer room we saw. It looked very primitive, but may be useful." Park exited. "Zoë, can you uplink to a..." Thump.

"Park! Park!" called Richardson, "O'Ryan, what is going on?"

"I am checking it out." He came to the room where Park had come. A place in the floor revealed a hidden door, which he quietly climbed through and whispered, "I think she fell through this trap door. I see no sign of her...hold on. Listen!"

"So you are the infamous Park O'Ryan," came a thick Russian tongue. "You are not so much. I expected someone a little bigger. You are what my men are afraid of?"

"Gorshev. This whole assignment was a trick. Clever, I like a worthy opponent." She pulled her arms free from the two goons that had dragged her in.

"Park, location? Park! Get some back up in there,

now! Location, Park?" Richardson commanded.

"Sir," answered Zoë, "I think her ear piece is down. She does not respond. We can hear her, but she does not seem to hear us."

"O'Ryan, what is your location?"

Again, he whispered, "I have been able to hide in a small heating duct. I do not know how long I can remain, though."

"Hold position. Do not make a sound!" ordered the boss.

Gorshev had continued speaking, "She will have a partner. The rest of her team left, but there will be one more. Find him! Hanov, tie her up. This is even better than I hoped for," he turned to speak to her.

Park pulled her pistol from the thigh holster, taking three men out before Hanov knocked it from her hand.

Another henchman twisted a cable into a lasso beside

her, and as he let it go, it caught her arm. She let it tighten barely and pulled hard causing the man on the other end to lose balance. She wrapped the cord around his neck, until he stopped breathing.

Four more men were over her now with automatic weapons poking her back and head. She surrendered her hands to them.

"String her to that spike over there," ordered the cruel boss. His smiled showed that he was relishing in his victory, as she hung by her wrists a yard from the floor. "I could kill you, but that would be too easy. My brother should not have died. Now, you will pay for it. Continue, Hanov!"

The Great Escape

Hanov procured the tools of torture, but Park paid no heed. She was in a stare down with Gorshev. She was not even aware of the pain they were inflicting, for her anger had consumed any feeling. He watched her eyes for a minute and then questioned, "Why do you not fear me? I am going to kill you slowly and painfully and you show no fear?"

Park's words were strong from conviction. "I fear not what man can do. You can destroy the flesh, but you cannot send my soul to hell. You cannot dictate when I die. God has appointed that time, and until that appointed time, you cannot touch me."

"That is where you are wrong. I am God, for your life is in my control." He scoffed and made a motion with his hand. Hanov, show her how useless her God is."

Beating her did not make her succumb to their wishes; neither did the electric shock, which did weaken the vessel.

"I can see the room now, sir," Nicholas reported, barely audible. "There are five men with her now, and I do not know how many are looking for me."

"She can handle five, just hold your position, and be quiet," ordered Richardson.

"She is not going to cave," announced Hanov.

"Of course she would not cave. I have had a year to learn every detail about our Mrs. O'Ryan, here." He held a folder up proudly. "Her mother beat her severely as a child. Shall I show them what I am talking about, Mrs. O'Ryan?" He took a knife from the table and removed two buttons viscously. Then, he stopped. "No, that would not change anything. Her file states that she has two daughters. I think they deserve to meet their grandfather. He would love them very much." He threatened.

Nicholas did not grasp the insinuation, but he could see the fire in the captive's eyes. Anger filled him too, causing him to move ever so slightly in defense of his children. Too late did he realize his mistake. They heard his commotion.

"She will endure any pain we can give her, because she has had years to practice. Her weakness is her children and husband. We have already taken care of the latter." The inhuman creature proudly reported, and then the captors brought Nicholas in.

One of the henchman announced, "Look what we found."

"Well, well, look who we have here. Mr. O'Ryan, nice to see you again. We are glad you could join us for this momentous occasion."

Park wheeled her head. They detected him. Why didn't he get out? She could not have him hurt anymore.

They pushed Nicholas with the ends of the automatic weapons. He wore an angry expression and refused to look at the one he let down.

"Should we look for more?"

Gorshev answered, "No. There will be no more. Hanov, you wanted to see fear in her eyes? Now, you have fear."

While his men mocked her, she awaited the perfect moment to make her move. It was almost here.

There it was! Gorshev had backed just far enough for her legs to reach him, and she wrapped the strong limbs around his neck, pushed herself up briefly, and unlatched the cable from the spike. In one swift graceful move, she rolled frontward, broke Gorshev's neck with her bonds, grabbed his gun, and shot the two men holding Nicholas.

Nicholas wasted no time. He pulled the dead man's gun on the other two men. The partner team disarmed each of the bodies. Nicholas swiftly loosed her binds and they proceeded to egress with the surviving rebels leading.

Nicholas awakened to a completely new world that

night in understanding that his stranger-wife belonged in a realm where few could go. The great escape immortalized her in his opinion.

The Decision

Park and Nicholas finished the night in bunkrooms at the headquarters because of the late hour in which they returned and the fact that Park had to have medical attention for a dislocated shoulder.

The following morning, Nicholas still high from the adrenaline rush of the narrow escape, bragged to Fred how wonderful Park performed.

"You should have seen it. It was amazing. She had three men down before I was able to think clear enough to react," he was saying.

"I have seen her in action, my friend. That is why they consider her the best. You were just as good as her before, well, you know." Park came out of Richardson's office. Nicholas watched her glide to her destination, as a smile conquering his lips. "Talk about déjà vu," Fred was saying.

"Excuse me?"

Fred spread his big grin, "You were in that same spot when she walked into Richardson's office the first time you ever saw her, and you had that same look on your mug."

Nicholas stood up in eager pleasure, because she was approaching. "Are you going home?" She asked.

"Yeah, I was waiting on Fred to give me a ride."

"I can give you a lift, if that is alright?" She offered.

"Of course." He was ready to follow her.

"I'll meet you at the Jeep. I have to do one more thing before I go. Bye, Fred." She kissed his cheek and was gone.

"Hey Nicholas," he called after the agent, "Precious is a good girl. She's seen enough suffering to last two lifetimes, and I don't intend to see her hurt anymore."

Nicholas considered the stern warning, "I understand."

Park did not take him to their house. She drove to a house up the beach two blocks from their house while refusing to answer his questions until they were inside. When she did explain, he was bewildered.

"Do you like this house?" she asked.

"It is fine, why?"

"Because, it is yours." He stared at her in disbelief. "I bought it for you. It is close enough to the house that you can see Sarah and Anna anytime. We want you to come over and spend time. We are not pushing you out of our lives, so I do not want you to think that."

He angered, "Sounds to me like that is exactly what *you* are doing. What is this all about?"

She handed him some papers, "I want you to sign these."

"Divorce papers?" he retorted after skimming them.

"It is better this way."

Nicholas gathered her up in his strong embrace. His boyish mind was unable to function clear, and with all the passion inside, he kissed her. "I love you. Can you not feel it?" he mumbled.

It Is Over

For the brevity of a moment, Park forgot her position and reasons for being here and reciprocated that passion. "No!" she pushed him away. "You do not know what love is."

"Yes, I do."

"No, you have not matured enough to understand what it really is. Since the accident, you have been a little boy in a man's body. You think you love me because I am all you know. You have not had the opportunity to experience a relationship with other women. You feel this way, because everyone told you this is how you feel. I am a safety net to you. When you are in trouble, I am the safe one. That is all you know."

"That is not true," he protested.

"Who else have you been with? I mean who else have you thought about in a romantic way?"

"I do not understand why you have to do this divorce."

"Nicholas, if you love me the way you think you do, then waiting a year or two will not make a difference. What if your feelings are just an infatuation, a hero worship type of thing and I hold you bound to this marriage? Three years down the road, you find out that I was not what you expected, and you want someone else. Is that fair to the girls, to you, to me?"

"That is not going to happen."

"You have no guarantees, Nick. You cannot promise me life lasting love, because you do not know me any more."

"Then I would be better off to have been killed that day." Seeing his words cut to her heart, he regretted them as soon as they came out. "I am sorry. I should not have said that."

"Don't be sorry for how you feel. I will not trap you

in a marriage where you will learn to hate me, because I took away your past, your children, your dad…"

He looked at her questioningly, "Why would I blame you?"

"Because, it is my fault!"

"How? Did you inject me with that drug? Did you hold me prisoner?"

"What I did was much worse. God tested me and I failed. If I had not failed God, you would not be like this today."

"You confuse me. I don't understand."

"They grabbed you. Gorshev told me you were dead. I let hatred kill Gorshev instead of letting God work His way. You would still have been safe, had I not killed him. He could have bargained with you and you would never have suffered through this."

The guilt in her voice stopped his argument. He

didn't see it that way, but he did not know how to fix it. He turned so he would not have to see her face. He was confused.

"Sign the papers, Nick. You will find that I have been fair. I have redeemed all your property that you had before we were married, along with the plane and the house in North Carolina."

"I thought I gave them to you."

"I don't want anyone thinking I took advantage of you. I would not keep any of it. Here is your bankbook. There is no balance on the house. You should not need for anything."

"I don't want this. Please?" he begged.

Park was fighting the tears. She would not let him see them. "Nicholas, if you truly love me, I will be here. Take this time to date others and find out for sure if I am the one you want. Prove your love is real, wait a year or so and see if you feel the same."

124

The man reluctantly took a pen and signed the papers. "I will wait as you say I must, but I will not date other women. I will bide by your wishes, but I do not have to like it. In the end, you will find out how wrong you were about me."

"My house is still always open for you. Thanksgiving dinner and Christmas will be as usual. You will come for the sake of the girls at least, right?"

"Not just for the girls, Park. You may be able to dictate your non-marriage to me, but you cannot dictate my heart."

Park left quickly, saying, "You can pick up your belongings any time." She put her hand to stop her heart from pounding out of her chest. This was the hardest thing she ever had to do. Her flesh yearned to run back in and recant it all, and say, "I love you, and I will take you any way I can get you," but she knew this was the wrong thing to do.

Overworked

Teaching would not begin until after the beginning of the year, and Park was trying to be home more for her girls. They had so much to adjust to in the last few years, that she just wanted them to feel safe.

Park had signed over her bank account to Nicholas in the settlement. She did not want any of the money earned in exchange for his life. She regretted not having more to give him.

In order to make up for the lack of income, she took on some bookkeeping for a large company to earn extra money.

The week of Thanksgiving came, bringing the Kansas loved ones for the week. They would stay in the new addition over the garage that Nicholas and Park had built. It was awkward with Nicholas living in another house, but he spent much of that week with his girls at their home.

Pop objected to Park divorcing his son but tried to understand Park's view of things, realizing it was in his son's best interest did not make him like it any better. It was just plain wrong to put a finality to a sacred union.

The week of Thanksgiving gave him opportunity to confide in his son that Park was acting strange. She spent most days at home in the study, working all hours of the night, but on what he did not know. Circles formed around her eyes from lack of sleep, and she insisted on taking more work.

Park had to have the accounting job she was working on completed by the end of the month, which was only four days away. The good news was that she was almost finished. That Wednesday night, she flitted between kitchen and study after everyone had retired, thinking that she should be able finish, if she worked through tomorrow night also.

When Thursday morning dawned, Pop found his little

girl slumped over her desk in exhaustion. "Little girl," he spoke softly, "why don't you go get some sleep in the bed?"

She lifted her weary head, "I have to finish this. I'll go in a few minutes." She massaged her temples.

"You have worked yourself into another migraine. What is this you are doing? I can finish this while you go rest."

"I will be okay. Just let me shower and I'll be refreshed." She skipped up to her room.

Pop disappointedly retreated to the kitchen, where Kathy was preparing breakfast. He kissed her cheek and sat at the table with a cup of coffee. "Good morning, Pumpkin."

"Good morning, Daddy. Did you sleep well?"

"Just fine. I am…"

A knock on the back door interrupted, and Sarah and

Anna came in rubbing the sleep from their eyes.

Anna ran to her Dad's arms upon seeing him at the door, "Daddy! Happy Thanksgiving. Are you going to eat turkey?"

"If it tastes anything like it smells, I am," he received his kiss. "Good morning, Sarah."

"Good morning, Daddy," he received a second kiss from the reserved daughter.

"Where's Momma?" asked Anna.

"Upstairs in the shower," said Grandpa. "I worry about her. I found her asleep over that confounded computer a while ago. She woke up with a headache. She is going to keep it up and end up in the hospital again."

"She does not take her pills anymore," informed Sarah as if she were an adult.

The grandfather turned to Sarah, "How do you know?"

"Cause, the bottle has been empty for over a week, now."

"Sarah, how come you didn't tell your dad or me?" asked Grandpa kindly. "You know Momma has to take them to stay healthy,"

"Momma said she'd get it refilled and start taking it again, but she kept forgetting," she defended.

Anna looked at her father with trusting eyes, "Daddy, is she getting sick again?"

Nicholas did not know how to respond. He looked at his father for help.

"Anna, you have Daddy, me, Bruce, Kathy, Fred, and Christy. We will not let anything happen to your Momma," the old man smiled with a pat on her head.

"Good, what time is dinner?" asked Hazel.

"One o'clock," chimed in Kathy. "Hazel, don't eat the pie for breakfast."

"Come on Hazel, we will go to the playroom," invited her cousin.

Nicholas looked at his father. "Is her medicine serious?"

"When they told her you were dead, her little heart could not handle the anxiety of losing you. She suffered a small heart attack. The medicine is to keep it relaxed."

"Then, she needs to take it?"

Kathy asked curiously, "Dad, what is she doing in the study all the time?"

"She is doing some accounting for some big company."

"Accounting?" asked Nicholas.

Kathy questioned, "Why is she moonlighting, Nicky?"

Nicholas was just as confused as they were. "I don't know. In case you forgot, she does not share with me."

Park came into the kitchen feeling somewhat refreshed, "What? Why is everybody looking at me like that?"

"You are just paranoid, sister dear. How come you didn't leave a whole lot for me to do?" Kathy accused. "I got up this morning expecting to accomplish a lot of cooking; only to find out you have done most of it."

Park laughed, "I got absorbed in what I was doing, and didn't realize I had finished all this. Come on, we can finish the rest."

For the rest of the morning, Pop and Nicholas watched in silence from the den under the pretense of watching a ball game.

Reassessing

While the women were removing the dishes from the table, the phone rang. Park excused herself to the study to answer.

"Hello." The two watchdogs heard through the open door.

A friendly voice came over the phone, "Hi Park, guess what?"

"Shawn! Is it benefit time again?" She laughed.

"You got it! Can I expect you there?"

Park thought briefly, and then lowered her tone, while pushing the door closed with her foot. "Listen, do you think you can find a really nice girl to take Nicholas to the benefit?"

Shawn Grayson was not sure of this most unusual

request, but anything for Park suited him. "Sure, I have a cousin, why?"

"I will explain later. Oh, and I thought of something else."

"What is that?" Shawn Grayson asked.

"What if we fix up your mother and Pop to go together? They would really like each other," she plotted wickedly.

"Sounds good to me, but if your date is taken and mine is taken, that means we have to go together."

"What is the date this year?"

"The seventeenth."

Park hung up after answering, "I will expect to see you then." She picked up the receiver again. "Hank, are you still interested in buying *Dixie's Pride* for your med chopper?"

"Shoot yeah," replied the excited voice of Hank. "I thought you'd never sell her."

"Pick up the papers and keys today. I trust you to be fair."

"I'll be there by four o'clock."

"See you then."

She hated to sell Matt's gift to her, but she had to have cash for the tickets as well as the annual contribution to the benefit. They depended on every donation. She would be humiliated not to have a contribution. Hank had been pestering her to buy the chopper for years, and this would work out nicely.

Well, she might as well get the rest over with while she was at it. Once again, she lifted the phone to her ear and dialed. "Mr. Johnson, this is Park O'Ryan. You made an offer to buy Spirit a while back. Are you still interested?"

"Park, are you pulling my leg? You really will part

with Spirit?"

"I will sell him to you under two conditions. First, you can tell no one about it. Second, payment will be board and training for Pegasus and Triad for the next year."

"Park, I am taking advantage of you. I don't feel right doing that."

"Those are the conditions, Mr. Johnson. You will actually be doing me a favor," she excused.

"It's a deal. Do you need anything else?"

"That is all. Happy Thanksgiving, Mr. Johnson."

"You too Park, good bye."

Park's head was pounding every amplified beat of her heart. She would just sit down for a minute and then go help Kathy finish the dishes. She sat in her chair, but before she knew it she was into her bookkeeping again. Here, she remained until Nicholas knocked on the door with a man to see her.

"Hank, come on in," she smiled her charm weakly.

"Park check this out and make sure it's fair," said the man handing her a check.

Park grew annoyed that he had spoken before Nicholas had cleared the room. She did not bother to look at the paper in her hand. "I am sure it is." In turn, she handed him an envelope, "Here is everything you need. I apologize for asking you to do this on Thanksgiving."

"It was worth it." He turned to leave. "Nicholas, it is good to see you again."

Nicholas stared at the man leaving, oblivious to his identity. He was another memory lost forever.

Park hurried Hank to the front door in hopes of getting Nicholas out of her study. When she reentered, much to her chagrin, he was standing behind her desk.

Flaring Temper

"Park, why are you accounting for this medical company? Haven't your other two jobs taken enough of your time, that you need another?"

She tried to charm him with a sweet smile, "I am just helping out a friend, Nick. It is no big deal. I will be finished tomorrow and that will be the end of it."

"Helping out a friend, huh?" He went over and shut the door. "If helping out a friend is making you suffer, then he is not much of a friend."

"I am perfectly fine," she protested.

"Fine? Do you think we are all blind? Do you think we can't see how thin you are or how you've not slept in days. Look at the circles around your eyes. You look old. This is fine to you?" He inadvertently elevated his voice.

"Nicholas O'Ryan, do not stand in my house and raise your voice to me. Our children are upstairs and can hear," she did not realize how loud she had become. How dare he come in here and yell at her? He had no rights to her anymore. "I will thank you to mind your own business." She approached him, but the boiling blood pulsing through her veins rushed to her tired brain causing her to stagger with dizziness.

He was quick to swoop her small frame up quietly and open the door that led upstairs. She was not aware that she was holding her chest vehemently.

"Put me down!" she argued. "I am perfectly capable of walking. Nick, put me down."

He demonstrated an equal stubbornness by placing her on the bed and pulling the covers over her as if she were a child, which angered her yet more. When she tried to get up, he forcibly held her down. A challenge flashed across his features. He determined that if she never spoke to him again, he would win this battle.

"You are not going anywhere. I will stay here as long as necessary, but you are not getting up, and that is

139

final."

Park rose to protest, but a sharp pain put forth its might in her chest causing her to fall helplessly back. There was no point in arguing. She would appease him and lay down for a little, and then slip down and finish her job, when he took leave. She closed her eyes to fake her resting, but before she knew it, fell into a deep slumber.

The estranged husband looked at her peaceful sleeping form. Why did she have to be so incredibly stubborn? He was fighting an uphill battle with her. He had hoped that when she left with those divorce papers she would come to her senses.

Then a thought came to him. What if the reason she did not want him was that he wasn't a man anymore? He resolved to work harder to become the man she knew before. He would put his complete energy into this end. He would make her proud of him again.

Why couldn't she be as submissive awake as she was asleep? Look at her; she was precious to him, why could she not see that? She thought he didn't know how to love? He may have forgotten memories, but he was not stupid. He would show her. He would comply with all her requests. In the end, he would be in her heart.

He left her sleeping body and descended the stairs. The family tried not to look at him in indifference, but they had heard the raised voices.

He looked at one then another, "Dad, what is going on here? You live here, don't you know anything?"

The father responded, "Son, she is very private, she doesn't let me know her personal business. Maybe Bruce knows."

"He is in the mountains for the holidays. Besides, she would be furious to find out if we did that."

Kathy interjected, "We are four intelligent minds. Can't we figure this out ourselves?"

"Kathy is right. What did you find out, Son?" started Pop.

"First thing we do is get her started back on her medicine," Nicholas thought aloud.

"That is curious," said his father, "one time she stopped taking it on purpose. She said she did not need it, but I talked her into keeping up with it. She promised."

Nicholas slipped into the study to find a drug store that was open. They told him he could pick up the refill before eight o'clock.

Putting the facts together, he tried to figure out why his wife was doing this to herself. Thinking back to the conversation they had the day she brought him the divorce papers, he deduced. She was punishing herself, because she felt responsible for what happened to him.

How could he make her understand? It was not her fault.

Set Up

With Park completing the accounting job, selling *Dixie's Pride* and Spirit, and working her regular job, her finances became less burdensome. Regulated in her medicine again, she began growing stronger.

Nicholas kept a regular vigil on the house by way of the beach. Whenever he was not on assignments, he would stroll the beach to catch a vision of her through a window, or out on the ocean side with her hair blowing and appearing untouchable.

The month proceeded toward the surprise dates Park had planned for Pop and Nick. She knew Nicholas would not willingly do it on his own, so she was encouraging the plans for him to date others.

Her heart would always belong to Nick, her Nick, but he was not her Nick anymore. She longed to take him away to seclusion and live happily ever after, but her husband had died on that assignment. Her longing for him to remember his love for her overwhelmed her good sense sometimes. "God, I know this is my entire fault, and I deserve punishment for my sins. I ask you to give me grace to endure what I cannot bear. Give me Thy wisdom in all things. Do not let me choose to please the flesh, but to please Thee," became her fervent prayer. She knew God was in charge of her life now. Divorce was wrong, but this was unique circumstance.

As for Pop's secret set up, she felt that he had sacrificed his retirement to her and the girls. It was time he enjoyed a healthy full life without her depending so much on him. Mrs. Grayson was a sweet widow and deserved a little joy as well.

To her delight, he seemed pleased when she announced the surprise. Telling him had been so easy that she decided to volunteer him to tell Nicholas about his date. He only frowned heavily at the news.

Nicholas revolted, but then realizing he could satisfy Park's desire for him to get out and date, he agreed. He

144

realized where his destination lay, and if this was how to achieve it, so be it. He did not hesitate to vocalize how much he disapproved of the setup and this Shawn character. What kind of man moved in on a married woman?

The night came for him to find out what kind of man Shawn was. A very handsomely dressed Nicholas arrived and nervously searched for a chance to speak to his dad alone. He wanted to back out. He did not think he could do this. The chance never arose for him to be alone, because Park doted on perfecting the kindly older gentleman's appearance, until the doorbell rang.

Shawn's cousin, Gerry, was a lovely woman indeed. Her beauty and money found her many willing candidates for husband, but the money always seemed to win out in the end, leaving the princess a bachelorette. Tonight, she wore a priceless red satin dress with pearl accessories. She was beautiful.

Pop went to the flower shop earlier and bought the usual daisy bouquet for Park to arrange in her own uniqueness, as well as a white corsage for Martha and Gerry. As the hostess pinned the lovely rose corsage on Nicholas's date, she perceived the loveliness in this girl. She was pleased with Shawn's choice of dates for Nicholas. Now he could see there were other nice, beautiful people in the world from whom he could choose.

Martha Grayson had put away her mourning clothes, and replaced them with a green velvet gown, causing Pop's eyes to twinkle with delight, as he pinned her corsage to the velvet. The twosome made an adorable couple.

Park acknowledged how dashing Shawn looked on the arm of his mother. She noticed Nicholas's ability to take her breath away. She dared not admit, even to herself, that he was incredible. She must keep these painful desires in check. He was not her Nicholas.

Park slipped upstairs to throw on the white cotton dress Nicholas had given to her in Montana. Getting through this evening was the only objective on her mind, so she did not care about looking good. She swiftly clipped a few of the white and yellow flowers in her loose hair and descended the stairs in less than a five-minute span.

Shawn declared, "You are the picture of an angel, Park. How do you do it?"

"Yes dear, and so quickly?" added Mrs. Grayson. "It takes me hours to look like this, and you were only gone five minutes."

Park blushed, "Are we ready?"

"I believe so," said her adoring escort.

Getting No Satisfaction

Since his dad's death, Shawn had become the chairman of the POW benefit. He schmoozed the crowd until they had all the pledges in for this year. His lean body had toned in the last year, filling out his tuxedo quite handsomely. He was as charming outside as he was inside.

Park was happy that Gerry and Martha seemed to be getting along with their dates. This aided in making Park's decision easier. Nicholas needed her out of his life, in order to get on with it.

To her ultimate surprise, Paul attended the benefit this year. Normally, he did not come to these functions. It was the first time since introducing Park to Mr. Grayson that he had come.

His perfect handsome smile greeted his former girlfriend. "I thought I might see you here."

"It has been a long time Paul. How have you been?"

Paul shook his head, "I have been doing really well. How about you? I heard about you and Nick getting married. How are the girls?"

"The girls are great. They would have loved to see you tonight."

"They are good kids. Maybe I will see them soon. He grew excited, "I met a woman that I fell in love with. Teresa and I are getting married. She is wonderful. I don't seem to have that jealousy problem with her that I had with you. Thank goodness."

The old charmed smile flashed, "I am so glad for you. You would probably never have been happy with me. God works all things out for His own purpose."

"I heard about what happened to your husband. I hate it. That is a downfall to being a doctor. We have the power to save lives, but unable to save them all. We want to cure every person we come across, but can't."

"It was not the will of the Lord for him to be cured

Paul. We have to accept that."

"Still, it must be very hard on you. I remember the way you looked at him. I knew you would never look at me that way. That day on your deck, he stood there telling me off with that same look in his eye. I knew then that you couldn't help being in love with him. If I thought for one minute that you would someday look at me like that, I would have waited forever."

"Now, you do have someone who will look at you that way."

He responded, "Yes."

Shawn came to claim his date. He shook hands with Paul, because he knew his dad liked him so well.

That was the last time she ever saw Paul again, thus closing a chapter in her forgotten past.

Over the next few weeks, Park realized that Nicholas

did not have eyes for Gerry or any of the other diverse women she placed upon him for exploring his options. His heart sealed with the fate of his forbidden love. These other women were good to look upon and kind as could be, but they could not fill the void that only his not-so-stranger wife could fill.

When the New Year rang in and Nicholas still did not desire to get on with his life, Park realized that as long as she was around, he never would. She knew that she would have to leave in order for him to put forth an effort.

She had a commitment with Kincaid to train pilots, but when that was over, she had already spoken to Richardson about sending her on an extra long assignment.

This would give father and son, as well as father and daughters, the time they so desperately needed to reconnect in love. He could devote full time to the girls. They needed their daddy back. "Yes," Park thought, "that is the most logical step to take."

151

Nicholas hesitantly agreed to move in with the girls, because he did not want Park to leave on this assignment. He knew this assignment was going to be different. She had never asked him to move into the house before. Even more bizarre, she refused to tell him when she would get back.

The assignment included her becoming a substitute teacher in a northern city school for about ten months. It was more of a police assignment than a secret agent assignment, but that did not matter to her. She was simply glad that she would be far away for a long period.

Child's Play

Jessica Simmons, AKA Park O'Ryan, infiltrated the school with a bang. She let the students know up front, she would take none of their shenanigans. She proved she could hold her own with these punks.

One of her first acts as teacher was to expel a boy for selling drugs in class, violent temper attacks on other students, theft, and property destruction. His infuriated mother faced off with Jessica Simmons, only to return home with a more knowledgeable picture of what her son really was.

For the most part, the students loved their new teacher. The ones that wanted to learn were actually learning for the first time in years. They had someone who cared about ensuring their education.

Ricky, a mature sixteen-year old, became one of her protégés. He was smart enough to be in the honors class, but peer pressure held him back. The unfortunate part of his story was that he had enough of his foot in a gang's door to cause trouble.

Park spent months pulling the young Ricky toward the side of education. If he would just concentrate on his studies, he could go to Harvard, and make a real difference to his community. Ricky failed to have the one requirement needed to fit in with the gangs, hate. His redemption lay in his love for fellow man. When the opportunity arose, outside of the school setting, Park witnessed to the youth, and came close to seeing him surrender his all to the Lord, but he did not.

Meanwhile, Alex, the youth Park expelled at the beginning of her stint, tried his best to corrupt young Ricky. He had his watchdogs spying on the new teacher to find out how he could get even with her. She had cut into his livelihood, and that was not tolerable.

Of course, Alex was not going to let his pawn know how he was using him, so he made his hold on Ricky sure. Ricky would brag on the teacher without knowing he was keeping Alex informed of her every move.

He deceived the vulnerable young man into a sense of nonviolence. Behind the scenes, though, he was committing atrocities. He could not tip his hand, or he would lose his pawn for good.

The other gang members did not like the partiality their leader showed to the new guy. They had to rob someone at gunpoint to become members, but this kid had no initiation at all. He just seemed to hang out with them. That wasn't fair.

When the nosy teacher busted one of Alex's cohorts for dealing on school property, he became enraged even more. The ten months since he had been out of school had given his hatred enough time to simmer. He had one goal in mind and only one.

To fulfill his wish, he charged one of the new recruits that she was his target for initiation, but he upped the stakes. He did not want the woman to walk away from her mugging.

When the moment came, the young man failed

155

miserably. He was no match for a trained agent. However, he went to jail showing loyalty to his gangster leader. He never revealed any information about the gang.

Jessica managed to keep Ricky from joining the gang and almost had him convinced to stay completely away for any of the gang members, but Pain Master, as Alex referred to himself, determined even harder that Ricky should join.

It was time to teach Simmons an overdue lesson about minding her own business. If he couldn't take her out of the picture, he would do the next best thing. He'd take out Ricky and as many other students as he could.

Their crude weapons were stowed under coats, as the gang entered the schoolyard. Pushing this one and shoving another, they anxiously awaited their prey. The drugs coursing through their veins made them fearless, giving them the illusion of invincibility.

Several students reported the gang's presence to the principal, but Pain Master knew he would do nothing. He knew the principal was scared of his gang. Consequently, he called the cops and just waited.

They caught Ricky off guard as soon as he entered the schoolyard, but they decided not to kill him yet. They were waiting for the teacher to show up first.

One girl, breathless from running, explained to Ms. Simmons what she had seen. Park threw down her pencil and ran to the yard. She had her pistol, but these were children, and she could not use it on them.

She stealthily came to where the boys were manhandling Ricky and surveyed her options. The other students had scattered, but Park could see where five heaps lay in various places either injured or dead. She blinked at the sound of a gunshot into the air. She had to get to Ricky.

There were three other boys besides Alex. Each jabbed their own gun into Ricky. Alex sat on a picnic table laughing at his boys. It appeared he had an automatic rifle, but she did not think he had fired it yet.

Park placed a disabling bullet into two of the gang members, and the third ran off in fear. Alex jumped from the table, grabbed Ricky, and held the gun to him.

"Come out; come out wherever you are, Teacher." He mocked loudly. "If you don't want to see Ricky boy's brains scattered all over the place, you'll listen to me."

Park stepped into his view. "Okay, Alex. If it is me you want then let Ricky go."

"Put down your gun." He added an obscene name.

Park obeyed his command and slowly approached. Ricky appeared to be unharmed. She was within reach of him, when she heard the police sirens blaring loudly nearby.

This startled Alex. He dropped his hold on Ricky and began backing up, but he still held his gun on Ricky. "Come on, Teacher. You are going with me."

She obediently followed. As soon as she was able, she placed her body between Alex and Ricky, but Ricky was not going to let anything happen to his favorite teacher.

"Come on, Alex. You can't get away with this. The cops are all around you." He ran in front of the teacher.

Park did not take her eyes from Alex's finger. She did not even listen to his words. She could tell he was in an induced agitation. Just a little more...

"Put the gun down." An official voice came over the bullhorn.

That was the motivation he needed. Park saw the gunman's finger move and pushed the young scholar out of the way. With one squeeze of the trigger, enough bullets sprayed to do the job. Black engulfed her.

From behind, the police officers began firing on the young hoodlum. It was too late for him. Chaos ensued.

Two bullets had entered Park's body and fled the other side. The doctors removed three more surgically.

The fact that Jessica Simmons was a secret alias left an unidentified woman in the hospital with five bullet holes in and out of her body and deemed a lone person in the world.

A Little Rebuke Goes a Long Way

"It certainly is a tragedy for the young teacher that was shot down in a shooting at Central High School in New York today," came the voice of the newsperson over the television Sarah was watching. "It is reported that Jessica Simmons, a first year teacher, was caught in the crossfire between gangs today at Central High. Sources say that Alexander Bernard Shank, a.k.a. Pain Master arrived at school with three other members of his gang with the intentions of shooting rival gang members. Miss Simmons reportedly became a human shield for one of the targets."

The TV continued with its broadcast, but Pop was not listening. The picture in front of him looked familiar. Change the hair color, take away the glasses and makeup, and she could have been Park. He hurriedly called Nicholas from outside and dismissed Sarah cautiously.

161

"Look at that picture on the screen." Nicholas studied for a moment; Pop explained his alarm, "Isn't that our little girl?"

"Why is the picture on there?"

Pop turned the volume up to get an explanation. Nicholas committed to find out more from work.

Richardson reacted immediately. He went on assignment to fake Jessica Simmons's death, so that he could move Park to the local hospital to recuperate.

He did not want to risk having Nicholas snooping around. He had been satisfied that Nicholas had seemed to move on without his former wife over the last few months. He had given O'Ryan a new partner, and they seemed to be working great together. Why did Nicholas have to start questioning him about Park, again?

He knew he could not keep her family from her. He would allow them access once Park settled into the local hospital. For Nicholas, there was no verbal reassurance in the world that would satisfy him.

Wild horses could not keep Pop from the hospital, when his son reported that Park was there. She awoke the first time with his kind wrinkled face watching her. She tried to speak, but found the tubes in her mouth prevented it.

His voice was stern but loving as he softly rebuked. "I wonder what goes through that brain of yours sometimes. What is the meaning of going out and getting yourself shot? Do you ever stop and think about your children and husband?" Park blinked back her surprise. The older man shook his head. "I'm sorry to fuss at you in this condition Little Girl, but I don't know what else to say. We have been so worried about you. You disappeared for months, without any contact or letting the ones that love you know whether you were dead or alive, and then when we do hear something about you, from the television no less, you prove that you care nothing for your own life. Your children need you, but you do not seem to give a lick about their needs. It is time you start

163

putting those girls first. Now you get better fast and get home and take care of my grandchildren, and if I hear anymore nonsense on your part, I will turn you over my knee."

His reaction devastated Park. He spoke in truth and love, but Pop never became cross with anyone. He verbalized what she had been feeling. She could not get angry with him, because his love for the girls was genuine.

Nicholas's visit brought a twinkle to her eye. Her heart rejoiced when he told her that four months ago he had gotten saved. He revealed that God had allowed him a different view of the world. In his new birth, He revealed to the humble servant an affirmation of his love for only one woman. He left her to think on what he had said, before pressing her for a response.

Bruce arrived and shook his head at her with a, "For the first time in your life I have you where you can't argue, and I can say what I want," and a laugh. He held his rebuke for her since she had been through enough for the time being.

A New Lease on Life

As she progressed, they removed the tube from her throat. It would be a little while before they would remove the IVs. She would need extensive recovery.

Nicholas came one day to brave all odds and try to reconcile with his lover. He could not remember the way it was the first time around, which made this all so very awkward. He had given her time to think about the possibility, and when he proposed remarriage, he felt confident she would comply.

Park thought a lot about his words. Her tired worn body could not fight anymore. She knew there would be a few last assignments before she could pull out completely, but she had already conveyed to Richardson that she was retiring. It was time she hung up the old holster for the last time. Besides, he was saved now.

"That sounds nice," she concluded to Nicholas's proposition right before closing her eyes and drifting to sleep.

The excited agent ran immediately home to tell his family of his conquest. "She did not turn away from me," he explained to his dad. "I believe she still loves me."

Pop looked at his son in concern, "Son, she is vulnerable. You cannot take advantage of her, or she will only resent you in the end."

"If she will agree to marry me Dad, what more could I want?"

"Have you told her about…it?" Nicholas turned a shameful face away from his dad. The old man surmised, "I didn't think so. She has a right to know everything, Son. You have to be completely honest with her."

"I wish I had not been such a fool."

"The truth always has a nasty way of coming out, one way or the other. She will forgive this, but she will not forgive you for lying," concluded the father.

"I will tell her, when she is home. She is too fragile to hear it now."

With confirmation that the whole truth would come out soon, Pop went to visit his little girl again.

"Well look who's awake this morning," he placed the vase of flowers on the counter. "You are looking better this morning, Little Girl."

"I feel better, Pop. When do you think they will release me? I am ready to go."

He laughed, "Don't go getting in any hurry Little Girl. You get whole before you try to leave. Are you ready for some good news?"

"Indeed, I am. What is going on?"

He sat down beside her and took her hand in his old worn ones, "Martha and I are getting married. She has been such a joy, and I love her. We wanted to wait for you to come home before we did. You are here now, and I see no point in waiting. Will you do us the honor?

Martha wanted you to be maid of honor, or at least a bride's maid."

"Oh Pop, I am so happy for you. She is a wonderful lady and I know you will take good care of her. Of course, I will be there."

"Good! Does two weeks from Friday sound good to you?" he was elated with all the joys that had fallen into his long life.

She lowered her eyes shamefully. "Pop, I appreciate what you said to me before. It made me stop and really think. You are right. I have been very selfish. I told Richardson that I am retiring, so I will not be in dangerous situations much longer."

"Little girl, I was out of line speaking to you that way. I am so sorry for going off the handle like that, especially while you were in here. I am glad to hear you are retiring, but don't do it because of what I said."

"I am retiring precisely for what you said. It *is* high

time I start thinking about my children. They are the most important things to me, besides the Lord."

"So are we good again? Does that mean you will be in our wedding?"

"Try and stop me," she smiled.

"I would like to see someone try and stop you from anything," declared Bruce coming through the door. "I pity that person." He came to the bedside to greet his long time friend with a hug and kiss.

"I have my two fellows here with me. This is the best medicine in the world," teased the patient quietly.

Bruce's face sobered suddenly, "I am not here for a social call, Sweetie. I am here with some bad news for you, and maybe an early release."

"Bruce, something has happened, I can see it in your face," Park accused.

He crossed to the other side of the bed. "It is your

grandmother, Sweetie. Your Aunt Belle called trying to find you, thinking I could reach you somehow. They found her dead this morning, she just went to sleep and never woke up." He waited to comfort his friend.

"It was her appointed time," pronounced a saddened Park. "She lived a hard life, I am glad her passing from this life was peaceful."

At an early age, Park's grandparents tried to get the courts to give them custody of her. Instead, the courts threw her from pillar to post, because they deemed the couple too old to raise her. Truthfully, they were too poor. Park's grandfather had drunk away all his money in the earlier years, and her grandmother had worked her fingers to the bone trying to provide for her five children.

When Park became old enough to go to work, she set up an account for her grandmother and continually supplied money for whatever reasons the grandmother wanted to spend it. This secret was between grandmother and grandchild. No one ever knew the difference, not even her grandfather.

"The doctor said he would release you early if you promise to return in two weeks for a complete checkup," Bruce informed her, "so get your duds together, and we will go home and pack for the mountains."

"If it means getting rid of these IVs, I am all for it." She looked at a worried pop.

To Grandmother's House We Go

The mountains were still cool in March, but this time they had the chill of death upon them. The winter's dead had begun to bud new life.

Park, still recovering, preferred to stay at the house that she and Nicholas once owned together. Nicholas happily agreed to her staying in it any time she wanted.

Her aunts and cousins pounced upon the unsuspecting invalid with claws bared. They seemed to bicker and fight over trivial things, especially finances.

Nicholas watched Park's exasperated expressions as she watched the whole scene. Her fingers pressed tightly against her temples. He knew she was getting another migraine.

He quietly interjected for his former wife, "You need not worry about the expenses, ladies. Park and I will pay for everything."

They all stopped and stared at him in awe. Then one cousin stood up with indignation, "Well, I like that. You never cared to do anything for her when she was alive, and now you want to come in and take all the glory in her death. Park, or Mary, or whatever you want to call yourself, you are all of a sudden so high and mighty. Why didn't you help her when she needed it?"

Aunt Belle snorted, "Betty, I told you not to say anything about what I told you. You shouldn't say that about your cousin. You know she's out saving the world or some nonsense."

Park discreetly slipped from her chair and excused herself. She hobbled her way to a darkened bedroom to be alone. She realized this was going to be a difficult week. "Lord God, please give me strength," she prayed.

Bruce bit his tongue hard not to say anything to these busybodies. He knew he should not, because he was not family, but Nicholas didn't know any better.

173

"I will thank you not to come into my home, enjoy my hospitality, and insult my wife that way," he roared angrily. He hurriedly scribbled a check and thrust it at the women. "Here is a check for ten thousand dollars. That should more than suffice all funeral expenses. What is left over, keep it, but do not ever come in my house again with words against my family." He stormed out of the room, leaving the aunts and cousins speechless in awe.

When the phone rang, Bruce answered it for Park. It was a call for Aunt Janet. A few minutes later the old hen returned to her nest to cackle some more with the other hens. "Looks like we may need more than money to fix this one," she gloated.

"Why, what happened?" asked Cousin Trudy.

"That was Shelby. The funeral home called me. Seems like Mary's mother... oh I can't even say it."

"What did Abigail do this time?" snorted Aunt Belle. "God knows she has caused enough grief to last a lifetime for us all."

174

"Yes, but this one takes the cake," replied Aunt Janet, "it seems dear ole sis went to the funeral home with the body and demanded they bury her without any death certificate or anything. When the director refused, she threw mother, casket and all, in the back of the pickup and left. The director said as far as he knew, that is where the body still is.

"Unbelievable, absolutely unbelievable! Where did Mary go?" Aunt Belle reminded one of a pig, snorting every sentence she spoke. "Go find her Trudy, see what she has to say to this."

"What can we do? Could we hire a lawyer to make her give us back the body?" suggested Janet.

"She would have no choice," chimed in Betty.

Clucking Hens

Trudy had become fearful of Nicholas since his outburst, so she evaded the rooms he occupied. She slipped upstairs and found Park in the darkened room. "Park, Mom wants you to come back down. It's real important. Your mother has done it again, and we don't know what to do about it."

Park lifted a weary smile to her cousin, "It will be all right Trudy. Don't worry about a thing."

She followed the nervous cousin back downstairs, slowly and painfully. Her wounds remained sore. Nicholas happened to see her reentering the den of lions and followed himself.

"Well Mary, what are you planning to do about this?" asked Cousin Betty before she could even sit down. "She is your mother, how are you going to stop her?"

Nicholas watched Park try to smile her faint charm, "Whatever are you talking about Betty?"

Aunt Belle replied, "Your mother is carrying around your grandmother's body in the back of her pickup, refusing to let us bury her. Oh, the shame of it all!"

Park took on a look of embarrassment. Uncle Clyde arrived while Trudy was finding Park. He was a kind man with a brazen wife that had humbled him over the years of marriage. He was Abigail's brother, but he had severed all ties with the woman years ago. He respected his niece for the life she had overcome.

He jumped to her defense, "Betty, you can't hold Mary responsible for what her mother has done and I think you are being very unfair."

"Fair!" shrieked Janet, "You worry about fair? Tomorrow's front page of the newspaper is featuring this domestic dispute, and you are worried about us being fair to Mary?"

"Aunt Belle," Park began after some thought, "would you rather continue to fight in the public eye with this humiliation? I suggest we simply let Abigail bury her and let Grandmother rest in peace. Then we can mourn for her in a memorial service?"

Uncle Clyde stepped up again, "She's right Belle. Let Abigail do what she wants to do, we don't have to stoop to her level of thinking. We can have a service to remember Mother when Abigail is done."

"I just don't like it, that's all. It's not fair to us to be cheated out of a funeral," whined Aunt Belle.

"A lot of things in this life haven't been fair, Belle, to a lot of people. Park is a perfect example of that."

Park interrupted embarrassedly, "Uncle Clyde, that is a good idea. Will you call the funeral home and go over all the details. We can hold a service on Saturday. That will give them plenty of time to bury her and do their stuff."

"Sure Dumplin'. I'll take care of it. You don't look well, have you been sick?" the uncle asked.

"I am all right, Uncle Clyde, just a little tired."

"Then it's time we let you all get some rest. Come on Belle, Janet. Let's get out of their way."

"I still don't like it, Clyde. It should be us that buries her. We were the ones who took care of her all these years. No one else offered to help," protested the bully sister, as she threw an accusing glance at Park.

"Shut up, Belle," Park heard Clyde command.

Once the door closed, Park clumsily began to clean the dishes and mess that the guests had left. She was not sure how much the others had heard, and was somewhat embarrassed for them to know.

"What do you think you are doing?" Bruce fussed. "Christy and I will do these dishes. You go to bed."

Bruce and Christy pushed her to the side, refusing to let her continue. They demanded Nicholas take her to her room, where he waited for her to shower and ready herself for bed.

"You are still here?" asked Park, coming out of the

bathroom, fluffing her hair with the towel.

"I am not going to leave you till you are safe in bed."

She laughed, "Am I five again and need a father?"

"No, you are in desperate need of a husband."

"And you are applying for the job?" she put forth a weary smile.

"I do not have to stay in the guest room. I could stay in here with you and hold you until all your worries go away. You are not alone in this." The way he presented himself before her at this moment, it seemed like her old Nicholas standing there so handsome and caring.

"I am never alone Nicholas. I have a host of angels surrounding me, and I cannot stay with you because we are not married. You know that as well as I do."

"Then marry me tomorrow."

"Go to bed Nicholas. I will see you in the morning." She laughed softly, while she pushed him out the door.

Breaking Eggs

"I can't believe your mother has embarrassed us this way, Mary," Aunt Belle was telling Park over the phone Saturday morning. "Your Mother is as crazy as they come. You ought to have her locked up."

"Aunt Belle, I am sorry for what Abigail has done. I would take it all back if I could." Park softly disputed.

"Well if anything happens it'll be on your head, Mary Livingston," and with that she hung the phone up dramatically.

"Bruce, I am confused. Why does everyone keep calling Park, Mary? That is not her middle name. She told me she had no middle name." Nicholas questioned Bruce in another room.

"Someday, I will explain it to you brother. It is a long story. Let's see if the ladies are ready."

The sun refused to show itself for the memorial service. The dreary day was fitting for such an occasion. Park leaned into Nicholas's broad shoulder, for her pain was extreme. Her wounds were still painfully healing.

Some of the family and a couple of members from the church her grandmother attended came to the service, but it was no big affair. Few remnants remained of the family of Grace Jackson, beloved grandmother. If one can look from Heaven in the hereafter, she would have been tearful to see the events of the past week. It must not be true that they can see us from there, for the Bible says there are no tears in Heaven.

It took Park by surprise that Lisa came. It took several side-glances for Park to verify that it was really her. After all, it had been fifteen plus years since she had seen her last seen her sister. She carried a baby boy in her arms. Park assumed the child belonged to her sister. No one had mentioned her getting married.

The preacher motioned for all the guests to move in closer, so they could hear. They complied and the service began. He bowed his head and began to pray.

A gasp sounded throughout the silence, and then a baby began crying. When the eyes opened, Lisa lay on the ground, while red flooded around her limp body.

Park inexplicably drew to her side. Her feet moved without her knowledge. At her sister's side, she fell to her knees. Everything seemed to be in slow motion, while everyone threw themselves on the ground. Trudy was bleeding, now.

Park searched the scene for the cause of all this blood. A car screeched away from the church. Her gun was out of its holster, but no target was in sight. Quickly, she turned back to Lisa. Her pulse was weak, but she was alive.

"Nooooo!" Nicholas's tone was one that Park had never heard before. She left the 911 operator hanging, when she turned to Nicholas, who was cradling their Anna in his arms.

Her head was bleeding profusely. No one had seen the bullet pass through Nick's shoulder and rest in the bantam skull. She lay helpless in her Daddy's arms.

When the ambulance arrived, five people lay wounded from a lone sniper's rifle.

Anna's Ending

The doctors reported that Anna would never have use of her brain again. The bullet seared through the brain stem, causing her instant brain damage. Her body may continue to function, but she would never wake up again. It was up to the parents to decide whether they should unplug her life support system.

When the doctor returned for the parent's decision, he brought another surgeon with him. "Mr. O'Ryan, Mrs. O'Ryan, have you made your choice yet?"

"Stop her suffering Doctor," replied the bereaved father.

"That brings up another issue, then. This is Dr. Hangle. Mrs. O'Ryan, he is your sister's doctor. The bullet destroyed your sister's kidney. Being blood relations to Anna, we hope she would be a match f..."

"Take it," the bitter mother cried, "Whatever you need to keep anyone else from suffering at the hands of this monster. Just give me a few minutes with my Anna."

"Sure, Mrs. O'Ryan, I'll take you to I.C.U. so you can see her now."

Park requested her goodbyes to be private, void of even Nicholas. She climbed in bed beside her little girl and stroked the bandages that covered her red curls. The doctor's had performed surgery on her tiny head, and she could hardly see her angel's face. Her fingers gently touched the sweet swollen angelic features of her precious baby girl, as tears slowly emerged.

"My sweet little Anna. You have never known what you have meant to me. You were the last piece of Matt I ever had. You gave me life when I thought I would die. You were the sweetest angel I ever saw. Thank you for being a wonderful daughter all these years. I am so sorry I was not a good Momma to you and Sarah, and I hope you will forgive me for being away so much. I want you to go into Jesus's arms, now so your pain will stop. Your Nick Daddy loves you very much. You can tell your Matt Daddy how well he took care of us. You tell him not to worry about us, and we will see you soon. Anna Grace O'Ryan, you are giving your life that someone else might live, and that makes you a great hero. Take comfort in your walk through that valley in Jesus's bosom. He will carry you to Daddy."

The tears rolled across her nose and down the other side of her face. She pulled Anna's small hand to her lips. "I love you so much. I am so sorry I did not take better care of you." She heard a nurse stirring outside the curtain and wiped the tears away. "I will go and get Dad now, for I know how he would want to say goodbye to his little princess. You know he is going to have a rough time losing you. He has been with you from the day you were born. Sarah and I will have to try to help him through. Hold on for another minute. I will go get him."

Bruce and Christy sat in thought. What if that had been their Matt? They would not envy a mother and father losing their child this way. Their hearts cried out for their beloved friends.

They accompanied Nicholas back to the curtained

makeshift room, where they overheard the ending of Park's goodbye and cautiously came on in.

Bruce placed his hand on Park's head and kissed little Anna's oversized cheek. "Goodbye little one. You are heading for a better country. Tell Matt, I cannot wait to see him in his new clothes. I love you, Anna." He stopped for the tears choked his words.

Nicholas looked from wife to child without the ability to speak. He wrapped his unwounded arm around his little princess, and the two parents lay embraced with their little Anna, until the doctor came to take her away.

Pop had come to say his goodbyes, but seeing his son and daughter in their pitiful tragedy, he turned to leave them in privacy.

Roots of Wrath

Park refused to have the funeral in the mountains. She was ready to never step foot in this God-forsaken place again. She had learned with Nicholas's supposed death, not to resent God for taking away those whom she loved, yet it was hard to accept that He knew what was best for them all. It was hard to believe the death of such innocence could be best for anyone.

The funeral was a simple family affair, with Nicholas's kin and the Claytons in attendance. Richardson came, yet remained unseen. He was deeply saddened for his best agent, and complied all too quickly when Nicholas had come to him for help in dealing with the people responsible.

The casket lay to rest in its grave and Park turned her grief over to God, who enveloped her with a Peace that surpasses all understanding. She prayed for Nicholas to have that Peace about the little princess that had penetrated his heart.

Nicholas was angry at the monster that had snuffed out his Anna's life so carelessly. He wanted revenge, but he remembered what Park told him about the travails that fall upon you when you take things into your own hands instead of waiting for God. He remembered the suffering she said they all went through because of the revenge she took on Gorshev for the sake of revenge. The father who had just lost his daughter understood, in theory, but could not let this go with no repercussions.

The license plates of the escaping car proved who the gunman was. Richardson informed him that the shooter was Park's brother. Park had not offered any information about her family, so he could not understand how a brother could shoot his own sister, his niece, and other family members.

Abigail Livingston, in her unbalanced mind, had become infuriated that these people she hated so very much should dare to defy her and form a memorial for *her* mother. It was her way or no way, and her siblings, her

parents, and Mary Ann had defied her. That is why
Abigail, in her wrath, ordered Tim to take care of
business.

Tim was willing to go to the ends of the earth for his
mother. She had taught him the evils of this wicked
family and he genuinely hated them all, including his
sisters. Abigail had loads of money, acquired in nefarious
ways, in which she could buy Tim's allegiance, and he
was all too ready to earn it.

Lisa Livingston still refused to acknowledge her
sister, even after knowing Anna had saved her life. The
years of torment would not allow this woman to forgive
the sister that deserted her in her hell all those long years
ago. Park accepted this rejection because she never
expected any different from the start. She understood that
twenty years of disdain would not just disappear with a
kind act, not after Abigail Livingston finished with you.

Park buried Mary Ann with Anna. No longer would
she answer the calls from the loving aunts. She declared
herself dead to them with a vow never to come near them

again. Forgiveness was one thing, but stupidity was another. Death and destruction seemed to follow them wherever they went.

After finding out who killed little Anna, Park pleaded with Nick not to kill them. If he did, they would have no chance at ever being saved. "We have no right to dictate whether they go to hell or not," she argued.

Richardson played judge and jury on this case and kept from Park and Nicholas the punishment he bestowed upon the Livingston family.

Sarah was still relatively young, and could not express her grief the way Park could, so she bottled up losing her sister and kept it for another time. She had seen so much tragedy in her young life. Since she felt she could not turn to her mother, she learned to cling to her grandpa over the last little while, but now he was marrying and leaving.

She had cultivated antipathy through each tragedy with growing resentment toward Mom and Dad for letting

Anna get killed, resentment for her real dad for getting killed, and resentment for Grandpa for leaving her. Sonya had been the constant in her life, but she was too young to offer the proper help.

Pop's Wedding

Nicholas was not sure how to tell this secret to the woman he loved. He knew what he felt for her would never go away, even if she pushed him away for a thousand years. She held the key to his contentment. Furthermore, he was beginning to feel that it was his sins that caused Anna's premature death. It was retribution for what he had done. How could the mother of his dead child forgive him for causing her death?

Nicholas had packed up his house, so that they could give it to Pop and Martha for a wedding present. Park allowed Nicholas to stay on the couch. The secret he was hiding added a tension that Park did not understand. It made the living arrangements even more awkward.

The wedding took place on the beach up the coast near the Grayson mansion. There were four pillars placed with white sheets of sheer blowing gently in the breeze, while the silver bells chimed in time.

Pop never looked better in his tuxedo and Martha was an Egyptian queen. Shawn escorted her down the silver carpet to her new husband.

Pop graciously accepted the duties to love, honor, and cherish this woman for the rest of her life. Park had not seen him happier, except the time she told him she had found his long lost son.

Martha threw Park into a sweet yellow gown adorned with white and yellow roses. Even in her sadness, she still portrayed a sort of goddess. Shawn was enraptured with her, but the sad droop of her charmed smile made him repent that he should think her beautiful. He knew her heart would never be his. He never stood a chance with this exquisite creature, but he could not prevent his heart from falling.

She never encouraged his feelings, no matter how much he tried. There was an age difference, but Park was not the type to worry about that. He had hoped, when they thought Nick was dead, that he might have a chance but that did not happen. There she stood in all her pure glory,

195

untouchable and alluring.

Shawn was not the only one swept away. Even though grief still gripped his heart over their little princess, she fascinated Nicholas's soul. Anna's death placed a pall on his heart, but no time for comfort was afforded. Until he had cleared the air with the one to whom he wanted to share his life, he would not have complete peace.

They held the reception in the great Grayson mansion. Pop and Martha danced to the stringed orchestra the first dance of their married life. While Pop requested his next dance be with his grandgirl, Shawn waltzed with his mother before completely giving her to another man forever.

Nicholas and Park clave to each other in heart, mourning for their little Anna who was no more. They felt the relief, the pain, and the joy from all this time, hearing only the heartbeats of one another. Afraid to let go, Park held on to this moment for fear that her happiness might end as it always seemed to.

After the new Mr. and Mrs. McCrain left for the honeymoon, all the wedding guests drifted home.

"Sweetie," Bruce came up behind Park on the beach, when they reached her house, "why don't you spend some time in Montana? You could use the break. Maybe you and Nick can take a honeymoon trip of your own, and get the rest at the same time."

She kissed her long time friend on the cheek, her smile still faint, "You know Brother, I have always felt sorry for myself thinking I was all alone in the world, but I have a brother in Christ who has been there for me no matter what. I appreciate everything you have ever done for me, my friend. I may not give you your just dues here, but know in Heaven, you will be rewarded beyond measure."

He blushed, "I have done no more for you that you have returned to me sevenfold."

"I don't think I have ever seen you blush, Bruce Clayton," she laughed sadly. "You do not have to worry about me. I loved Anna, but I would not want her back here for anything, if I knew she would suffer in this life. I am at peace with her dying. It is living that I have a problem with."

"Well, now you will marry that big lug you love and everything will turn out a lot better," comforted Bruce. "Why do I feel you are holding back? You are going to marry Nick, aren't you?"

"It is not a matter of marrying Nick. I am just waiting for the other shoe to drop. Every time I find a spot of tranquility something goes wrong, and I have to start all over again. What is it going to be this time?"

"If you keep looking for it to happen, it will Sweetie. Enjoy the peace while you can."

"Am I interrupting?" questioned the approaching Nicholas.

"No you are not, Brother. Actually, the missus and I need to be going. Park, can Sarah spend the night with

Sonya tonight?" Bruce dropped his arm from his friend's shoulder and greeted Nicholas by pushing him closer to Park.

"If she wants to, that is fine with me. Nick?" Truthfully, Park was nervous with the absence of everyone but her and Nicholas in that house alone. In her mind she cried, "Lord, give me strength."

"I have no problem with that. She always enjoys your house," replied Nicholas.

Sarah gave her mom and dad goodbye kisses with an extra whisper to Dad. The moment had come when Nicholas knew he had to clean the slate. "I need help here God," he prayed silently.

The Truth Hurts

"Is there anywhere we could go and talk without any interruptions?" he began.

She mounted the back of his motorcycle and directed him to the hidden cave, where years ago he declared his love for her for the very first time. "You would not remember this place," she explained. "You told me you found it one day by accident, and it was the place you always came to be alone. You brought me here the night I messed up the Doherty case. Richardson was ready to fire me, and everything was in the pits. That was when... well, you would not remember. This is where you confessed you loved me which forced me to admit to myself how I felt about you."

He took her in his strong arms, "Then here is where I will renew my love for you as well."

Park suspected this was the reason he wanted to talk alone. After all her prayers and months of debating, she conceded that this was the Lord's will in her life. There was nothing standing in the way. Everything seemed to be coming together in that direction. "Nicholas…"

He interpolated, "There is something I must say, before you agree to marry me again." He fell humbly to his knees holding her waist, not to let her go. "I understand why you divorced me and forced me to experience life. I did meet other people and experience life, and you were right. Had we jumped back into our marriage back then, I would only have hurt you in the end. During this expedition, I have discovered one thing. God did not give you and me a love to last forever, but He did give us love. Not once, but twice have we found each other and fell in love beyond our control. I love you with all I am inside and shall never love another again."

Park was not sure of this uneasy feeling that a 'but' was getting ready to come. "I agree. We certainly have been blessed." She continued to stroke his dark hair, waiting for him to tell her the 'but'.

"Before Jesus saved me, I did not understand all of

this. I did something that I can never undo, and I pray you can forgive me as Christ has forgiven me. Ever since I woke up in the hospital, you were the only thing I knew. You were my whole world, and then you left me. I was scared. I had my dad, but things felt strained around him. They still do. He is expecting something from me that I can never give. Anyway, I turned to work for clarity." It was so hard to continue. Slowly he spoke in humiliation, "Richardson sent Tessa Jankowski and me to Belgium on an assignment. During our guise as man and wife, we sort of blurred the professional boundaries."

Park did not realize that her hand had stopped the soothing touch. She wanted to push away as she always did. She could forgive him of one little moment. She had been in missions before when the lines of reality became blurred. This was different, somehow. She could not stop her skin from cringing under his touch.

He still could not raise his head to look at her. "When we returned from the mission I lost all reasoning. I was frustrated with you for leaving me, and I did not understand my feelings for you. The confusion of it all just hit me all at once, and I did not care what happened to me. I did something regrettable that I wish I could take back. Park, please forgive me."

Building up the courage to look at her, he immediately regretted it. He could not bear what he saw. The betrayal in her eyes bore through him like a dagger. Her smile was gone, and the lines of unbelief replaced it.

"You fool!" she chided to herself. "You keep setting yourself up for this. When will you learn?" What was she supposed to say? What did he expect from her? Could she come to terms with his actions? After all, she had pushed him into this predicament.

At this moment, she did not care if she ever saw Nicholas O'Ryan again. She could forgive an innocent feeling while on assignment, but he had returned home and chosen to continue. "Just leave me alone!" her mind screamed.

Nicholas looked toward the ground again. His shame

was upon him. Park removed his hands from her waist and walked to the water's edge. She did not react, so he followed her silently.

"Nicholas, as God has forgiven me of my sins, I also forgive you. Now, will you please take me back to the house?"

He was crestfallen. She had forgiven him, but he knew she no longer wanted him. He had done that which was incomprehensible. He could not blame her. If he had found out she had been with another man, he would want to die.

Without a word, he rode her to the house, where she packed a few clothes in a bag, and announced that she was going to find a place to stay for a while. She vanished into the evening, leaving a guilty Nicholas destitute.

Something about Park

Bruce returned to the scene to find the house dark and Park's Jeep gone, so he was pleased with himself that his plan was working so well. He decided to go ahead and leave the flowers that Christy arranged. As he flicked the light switch, he almost had a heart attack.

"Brother, how come you are sitting in the dark? I figured you and Park were gone when I didn't see her Jeep. Don't tell me she got called in to work, I figured they would give her some time off."

"She didn't get called in," said Nicholas sadly. "I ran her off again."

Bruce settled beside Nicholas on the floor of the den, "What happened? I assumed the two of you would be off celebrating."

Nicholas watched the coaster he was absent-mindedly playing with, without looking at his friend. "A few months ago I did something stupid with another woman."

Bruce's eyebrow arched, "Say it ain't so, Brother."

"I was just trying to date like she insisted I do, when it went farther than I expected. I just lost all good sense, and I have no excuse."

"And you told her this?"

"I could not lead her into a marriage without knowing the truth. You should have seen her eyes. I can't forget that look of treason. I wish with all my might to be able to take it back."

"Mmmm," grunted the best friend, "that is too bad."

"She said she forgave me but can she really?"

Bruce mused for a moment, "Park is like a wild horse. In the wild, they run free, careless of the world around them. That is what makes them magnificent creatures. They remain spirited until you break them.

Once you break the wild horse, you break their spirit, and even if you return them to the wild, they will never be the same anymore. You have stolen their spirit."

"So I can count on never getting her back, now that I broke her spirit?"

"Park will come around, just give her time. She has to filter this through that screened heart before she can deal with it. She has been through so much worse."

"I don't want her to come around, if it means she is settling for me," Nicholas replied.

Bruce laughed, "She is not settling for you, Brother. She loves you. You have to understand the woman. Park will not stay where she was not wanted. At the first sign of someone not wanting her, she leaves. If I know her, she is kicking herself for it being her fault. She probably feels you rejected her."

Nicholas protested, "Rejected her? She was gone for months, I didn't know when or if she was coming home.

She gave me no hope of a future. What was I suppose to do?"

"I know, I know…women! You are supposed to be able to read their minds, and know how they feel," sympathized a comical Bruce. "Christy is the same way. I am supposed to know everything about her, automatically. If I don't, then I am not a thoughtful person. 'We have been married all these years, and you still do not know me'," he imitated his wife.

"Maybe I should leave her alone and get on with my life."

"Now Brother, think about Sarah. She deserves Mom and Dad together. She has been cheated out of parents her entire life. Does she not matter? Besides, there are wonderful advantages to being married. Matt loved her love of life. People respond to her joy. He told me when they went to restaurants, that the server would seat them at the best table, as long as Park was with him." He shook his head laughing at the memory. "Nick, our ladies bring wonderful benefits to our lives. I even get

Christy to handle all our ugly callers, because people tend to be nicer to beautiful women, than ugly men."

"She is beautiful," proclaimed Nicholas.

"Beautiful maybe, but at least my wife is not stubborn. I would rather have beautiful over stubborn any day," pointed out Bruce.

Nicholas lifted his head off his hands, "You think Park is stubborn too?"

"As a mule," laughed Bruce.

Nick grimaced, "I think I am getting somewhere with her, when she gets some hard-headed idea in her head and throws me back where I started."

Bruce took a longer time laughing this time, "It is the most infuriating thing in the world. I have known Park since she was ten, and she was the most stubborn kid I ever knew, even then."

"It is more than being stubborn. She gets close-minded on an idea, and there is no convincing her otherwise. What makes her that way?"

"It is called survival. You don't know the life she has lived. Don't be so quick to judge her."

"I do not mean to judge her. I just am so frustrated, because everyone knows every detail of my life and I know nothing. I have nothing to fight with. She has all my ammunition. I want to understand her but she keeps it all locked away."

"When I first met her, I couldn't help admiring her. She stood, with her fists up, in the middle of a gang of rough fellows. They just wanted to see her cry, and when she refused to be afraid of them, it made them mad enough to start punching her. She went around the circle staring each one down and refusing to let a tear surface. They were going to let her go if she had cried, but she wouldn't. She stole my heart, when she looked at me. It was all I could do not to cry myself. I took her to my mom, because they had bloodied her lip and blacked her eye. I asked Mom how a kid could get to be that tough, because

210

I wanted to be like that." He paused in remembrance.

"What did your Mother say?" asked the listener earnestly.

"She told me, 'Son, she has been in a war with the devil.' She bore scars on her back from where her mother beat her. Mom told me they were the result of years of toughening up and that I did not want to be tough like that.'"

"I have heard several people talk, so I deduced some things that might have happened. You told me in North Carolina that you would explain later. Bruce why does her family call her Mary?"

"Mary Ann Livingston is Park's birth name. When she was nine, she left home. When she was old enough, she changed her name. She tried to eradicate her past, but no matter how hard she tried, it continually haunted her. There is always someone wanting to dredge it back up. So you see, her way of surviving is by locking everyone out of her heart."

Everything About Park

Nicholas had so many questions, now that someone was willing to provide the answers. "The man that killed Anna is Park's brother, and the woman we gave Anna's kidney to was her sister, right?"

Bruce explained, "More or less. There was a twenty-year span where they had not laid eyes on her, until Tim subpoenaed Park in some bogus custody hearing. That woke the sleeping giant."

"What do you mean?"

"Park had locked away some horrific memories in a place where she could not remember them, but when Tim forced the custody hearing, he unleashed the beast. Her father had done some unspeakable things to her and her sister when they were little. Her survival method was to block it out. I am no doctor, but that is why she gets such awful headaches, I think."

"She has been through a lot."

"She may be the most stubborn person I know, but she is the most forgiving. She has the love of Jesus in her heart. That is why I know she will forgive you."

Nicholas realized he must not tell her he knew of these private things. He pushed for more answers. "Bruce, why did I love her so much, or should I ask why did she love me so much? From what I understand, she had a unique thing with her first husband. What made her fall for a nobody like me, after having a superman like him?"

Bruce laughed, "You're not a nobody, Brother. Park and Matt were definitely unique. She fell for Matt from nearly day one. She was in love with him all through her junior and senior year. Matt made me promise never to tell her that he always was in love with her too. He had a rough life himself, and didn't want to drag her into his problems. His mother died giving birth to him, and he never saw his dad. He had a rough time in the homes he was in, and he was not sure he could handle the one he and Park were at, until he was eighteen. He used to get jealous of the line of boys stringing along chasing Park. She only saw Matt." He smiled at the memory. "We all three graduated together before enlisting in the Air Force. After boot camp, Matt came to the realization that he could make her proud, and finally asked her out. They finished college in the Air Force and got married. They were married almost four years when he died. Park was nine months pregnant with Anna, and it totally devastated her. You brought her a lot of comfort during that time. You were everything she needed and grew to love. You were her partner on and off the job."

"I can't get her to tell me how she feels about anything. She is always guarded."

"True," agreed Bruce, "but that is just how she is. She'll not let you see her hurting. When we thought you were dead, she hibernated and shut everyone out. It was by chance Fred and I found her in time after her heart attack. She suffers in silence."

Nicholas sighed, "There is so much I want to learn about her. She seems to think that I can't care enough for

214

her to include me in her suffering."

"She will learn to lean on you again, in time. She has to find a way to tell you about her scars, and I would imagine that is not easy. She bares physical scars along with these emotional ones. Her own father brutally assaulted and mutilated her. After smacking her upside the head with a sawed off two by four, he anchored her to the floor with knives. To conclude his savagery, he gutted her and left her for dead. The damage was ghastly."

"I never imagined anything like that."

Bruce shook his head, "It cannot be me that tells you this. She has to tell you in her own way. Can you understand that need?"

The ex-husband nodded. "I think so. She has seen enough betrayal in her life, especially by me. I wish I knew the little things so that I could have a leg to stand on. For instance, when is her birthday, her favorite food and color?"

Bruce picked at a piece of the carpet. "Her birthday? Her birthday fell on the day Gorshev captured you, and we thought you were dead? We deliberately ignore that day, for her sake."

"Wow!" Nicholas shook his head in dismay. Neither spoke for a minute or two. Then he questioned, "You told me you admired and loved Park for your entire life almost. Why did you never fell for her, Bruce?"

After another moment of thought, Bruce answered, "I did fall in love with her, but not the way you think. Park was too surreal to be someone in which one could fall *in love*. She posed as this tower of strength that was superhuman and untouchable to a mere mortal, and I was unworthy to be in her presence. A type of hero worship, I guess you could say. I was in love with her as one would be in love with a movie star they know is beyond their realm. I love Park and that will never change. Through her silent witness, she turned me from the ugly world of crime that I was venturing in and introduced me to a better Way."

The two men continued talking into the early hours of morning. Nicholas learned things about Park O'Ryan that enabled him to understand the intensity of his actions.

The Loft

Park sat on the table at Fred's station waiting for him to deliver equipment to another agent. She had come to invite him to lunch again.

"Well, if it isn't the infamous, Park O'Ryan." A cool female voice interrupted her thoughts.

Park turned to Tessa and greeted the colleague with her charmed smile. "Tessa, how are you?"

The nemesis mocked, "If you are looking for Nick, he's not here. We have an assignment together."

Park softly drew her breath. She would not let this girl see that she bothered her at all. "I am not looking for Nicholas. I am waiting on Fred," Park summoned her sweetest voice, regardless of her annoyance.

The snake struck vindictively, "I'm not stupid, I know why you're really here, and I'll tell you what's more. He is mine. He doesn't want you anymore. He got over you the day he met me, so why don't you just stop chasing him?" Park's continuous smile angered Tessa more. "Besides, I can give him what he wants whereas you can't. He was with me last night, and if I have anything to do with it, he'll have that child he wants before long."

Park's mind raced. Nicholas had run to Tessa for comfort! There was more to this relationship than he told her. He must really feel something for this girl, because he had lied!

Jankowski relentlessly pushed, "Why don't you just let him go, he doesn't love you. You try to make him think he is obligated to you and your kid that isn't even his. How pathetic can...."

A deep throat cleared loudly, "Can I help you with something, Jankowski?" interrupted Fred.

"Yep. I need a nine mil and two clips." The girl still glared at Park, who refused to allow this girl see that she was angry beyond words. She froze a smile on her lips and remained silent.

"Here, now get out," demanded Fred as he shoved her equipment in her hand. He waited until she was completely gone, "Now, where to Precious? What are you in the mood for?"

"I am not very hungry. Where do you want to go? Are you ready?" Park tried not to change her demeanor. This girl had certainly rattled her cage, but she was too proud to let anyone know.

Fred tried to be cheerful, "I am starving. Let's go."

Fred heard nearly all the conversation that passed between the two women, but decided to keep it quiet. If Nicholas didn't have enough sense than to be with that witch last night, then Precious should not be the one that had to suffer the nasty details. He could not tell from her countenance that Tessa had tortured her very soul.

After lunch, the mother busied herself with house hunting. The search resulted in her renting a loft apartment. This was the answer to her prayers. It was not right for her to be with Nicholas.

Tessa said Nicholas were leaving on assignment, so knowing the house was empty she ran home to pack her belongings.

"Sarah, I found a cute loft apartment down on Wharf Street," the mother explained, when the little girl came home. "You will love it. It has a door that leads to the roof, where you and Sonya can have a hideout and everything."

"Why are we moving, Momma? Doesn't Dad like this house anymore?"

"Dad is not moving. He is staying here in the house. It will be just the two of us," she deliberately left the anger out of her tone.

The anger of several years broke the dam and flooded to the surface of Sarah's heart, "I am not leaving Daddy. I thought you were getting remarried, and we'd all be together?"

Park was frustrated, why did it always have to be a battle? She maintained control, "No, we are not marrying, and I have found another place, so he doesn't have to. Now, go pack your things."

"No!" rebutted the girl for the first time in her life to her mother, "I am not going anywhere with you. Why do you always run away, Mother?

You can't handle when you're wrong and take off. You go to work or Montana or anywhere to be alone. You don't want Daddy around, and you didn't want Anna and me around. Why can't you marry Dad, so we can be a family again? Why do you have to be so selfish? I hate you, and I wish you were not my mother. I will go live with Christy and Bruce. Christy can be my mother, and you can go live by yourself."

Park could not argue with her. She had not been much of a mother to Sarah or Anna. Furthermore, she was not going to force her only living child to move from the only home she had ever known and stay with her when she did not want to. She called Christy and asked her to pick up Sarah and keep her until Nicholas returned home. That was the best thing for Sarah right now.

Her Jeep was packed and ready to go when Christy came. Sarah scowled at her mother without kissing her goodbye and left. Christy wondered about the tensions but did not ask questions. She knew Sarah had a special bond with Bruce, and he would find out what was wrong.

Park moved to the loft with the essentials. She did not need to take much. She brought a few things belonging to Sarah in hopes that her daughter would forgive her in a couple of days and come over.

Gone Again

Nicholas was operating on little sleep and was angry at the world. It had been a long grueling task of waiting and watching on this assignment. He wearily flung one foot in front of the other toward his bike. Out of nowhere, a fist struck his masculine jaw jolting him out of his self-pity. He turned in bewilderment to find Fred standing there soothing his knuckles.

"I warned you not to hurt her, but you had to do it anyway," the older man fumed.

Nicholas rubbed his sore jaw, "Do you mind telling me what in the world you are talking about and why you hit me?"

"I told you I didn't intend to see her hurt again. I warned you, but you didn't listen." Fred defended of his precious little one.

"I repeat, what are you talking about?" Nicholas was genuinely confused.

Fred ranted, "Don't play dumb with me. Your girlfriend couldn't wait to rub it in her face how you are spending your nights with her. If you want that kind of girl, that is your business, but you keep her away from Precious."

Nicholas's anger rose, "What girl? I have not spent any nights with any girl, except Park and Sarah."

"If you need a kid so bad that you have to stoop to that level, then you are a fool, and if that is how little you think of Precious, you are not the man I thought you were."

"But I tell you, I don't know what you are talking about. What girlfriend are you talking about, I would like to know?" demanded the defensive Nicholas.

"Jankowski filled Park in on a few details that weren't very pretty." Fred turned; satisfied he had defended his Precious.

"Where is Park?"

"You are not going to hurt her any more." Fred returned to face him down before walking off without leaving room for rebuttal.

Nicholas stormed back into the headquarters to find Jankowski. Dragging her by the arm to a private place, he demanded in a low grave voice, "You leave my wife alone! I don't know what you said to her, but if you come near her again, I will make you pay."

She laughed in his face, "I should have known that bag of bones, little Miss Goody Two Shoes would come crying to you. She couldn't defend herself from a fly." Then changing her sarcasm to a pleading flirt, "Come on Nicky. Let's go get a bite to eat. We can talk about this over some drinks or something."

His eyes flared wild as he jerked her arm, "Leave her alone!" and stormed off. How could he have ever been attracted to this creature? Her true self unveiled to expose a wicked beast. How could he have ever done such a thing? What must Park think? He had to tell her the truth.

He raced home to plead for forgiveness one more time, but only found a note that Park left, explaining that she wanted him to keep the house and that Sarah preferred to live with him. She would not fight him for custody under the condition that he and Tessa hold off around Sarah until after they married.

After slamming a fist into the table, he called Bruce, who reluctantly gave him the address to her loft. Inexplicably, this angered him even more.

Nicholas got no response from his knock at the loft. Thinking she might be with Shawn, he shamefully gave him a call. Shawn informed him that he had spoken to her about business but had not seen her since the wedding. Where could she be?

When her Jeep was not in the drive for two days, he went to the base to plead help from Bruce. Bruce called Montana, but no one had seen her come or go there.

Before he left the base, they tried Bruce's hunch. The two men went to the hangar to find out if her chopper was gone. She would have to leave an itinerary, if she traveled by air.

Bruce took charge, "Hey Hopkins, I don't see O'Ryan's chopper around, may I see her itinerary?"

The man he had addressed as Hopkins stood puzzled. He looked at another man before answering, "Clayton, she didn't give me any flight schedule."

"What about you, Daniels?"

He too looked nervous, "She didn't leave any itinerary, because she didn't go anywhere. She hasn't been to the hangar in over a year."

"Then who is flying around in her plane?" asked the confused best friend.

"Uh, I figured you knew about her selling it," insinuated Daniels.

"Sold it! When?" Bruce looked at Nicholas in astonishment.

"She sold it, maybe two thanksgivings ago to Hank Johnson. I'm sorry, man, I thought you knew. I hope she doesn't kill me for telling you."

Bruce slapped him on the shoulder, "I'll not tell her I know. When she is ready for me to know, she will tell me. Thanks." The two friends walked back to the offices. "I don't understand why she would sell *Dixie's Pride*. She loved that bird. Matt bought it for her, and I can't see her parting with it for any reason."

Nicholas grimaced, "I believe I know one reason."

"Brother, you are holding out on me? Spill."

"Just between us?"

"Just between us," Bruce reassured.

"She ran into some financial troubles, when she divorced me. I think you were visiting your family for the holidays, and we found out she had taken on another job. I believe she gave me almost everything. What could I do? She refused to take any money from me. If I told her

I knew she needed help..."

Bruce interjected, "She would have your head on a silver platter. There is nothing worse than getting on her bad side."

"You are telling me."

"For now though, she will come back when she is ready. Give her time to lick her wounds."

Grieving

Park spent a week and a half in an enchanted lighthouse estate in Maine. Fred owned it and offered it as an escape for his Precious.

The first few days were the hardest for her. Her heart ached for her little girl. Anna loved the ocean. She would get so excited watching the ships pass by. Her little angel would have loved to come and sit in this lighthouse and spend all day. She had cheated her baby out of life and could lay the blame nowhere else.

Why did she not bring the girls here sooner? Why did she not bide Matt's wishes? Did he have the foreknowledge of his and Anna's death? Her beloved Matt, was he angry with her right now?

The Bible says to be angry and sin not, but she found that almost impossible. Her anger had festered inside for so long that Anna's murder seemed to be the straw that broke the camel's back. A flood of resentment

231

overwhelmed her, as thoughts of revenge consumed her.

She could make all those who had harmed her in the past go away for good. She could fix it to where they would never bother her or Lisa, or anyone ever again. She could...No! She could do nothing, especially ponder such thoughts.

It only took a fraction of a thought to encourage reaction. She must leave the revenge business to God. "Remember the last time you avenged for yourself?" Her brain yelled.

She cried out to Him for comfort. He was the only one that could help her at this point. Her beloved Matt, her darling child, even *her* Nicholas were dead and gone. If it were not for Sarah, she would throw herself from the top of this lighthouse and go be with her loved ones again. The only reason she needed to stay in this old place was Sarah and she did not want anything to do with Park.

She longed to hold her baby in her arms again. She could smell her sweet hair, blowing in the wind. She remembered her last little, "I love you, Mommy". Why did God need her more than she needed her? Why did He need to take her little angel?

Her physical wounds were healing faster than her emotional wounds. Just as she did with Nicholas, she would have to carry the guilt and responsibility of Anna's death for the rest of her life.

She did not even think about Nicholas's indiscretion for the first week. She really did not want to think about it at all. After all, she *had* told him to date other women. She had no right to be angry or hurt.

She prayed for God to show her wisdom, and He showed her beyond any doubt, that Nicholas had not returned to that woman. The flesh wanted to shift the blame on him, but she knew the truth. He told her it was over, and God affirmed it for her.

She forgave him in theory. Someday they could possibly have a friendship, but she was afraid to let herself love him again. "Please help me Father. Sometimes, I think my punishment is more than I can bear."

True to her nature, she pushed the pain deep in her heart and set about planning what was the best thing for them all. Like many times before, she laid the problem at the Fixer-upper's feet, and then picked it up again.

One Last Hoorah

Shawn had been working for over two years on another rescue mission. Time for execution was nearing. He had been talking to Park all along for help. She agreed to do it, but this would be the last time. This was to be her last mission of any sort. She began a regime of training to get into top physical condition after her injuries.

During her absence, she called Richardson to announce she would not be returning to her job. He understood her need to leave the Secret Service and complied readily. He even offered to help her and Sarah start over anywhere in the world with a clean slate.

Next, she called Kincaid who regretfully retired her from the Air Force. He offered his assistance also, for Matt's sake.

A plan was taking shape to take Sarah far away and start afresh. She would never look at this life again. She completed her duty and served her country, but now she must serve what was left of her family. She must take care of Sarah's needs. Sarah was the most important thing in her life.

When Park returned home, she called Sarah to come visit her, but Sarah was still too angry to comply. "She's finally home, Dad," she told her father.

"Your mom is home?" he asked hopefully.

"I don't see why you should care. She doesn't care enough about us to stay here and marry you," stated the angry girl.

"Sarah, don't talk that way about your mother. She is right for not marrying me right now. She has her reasons," he defended.

"Reasons? She always has reasons. She has reasons for not marrying you, reasons for not living with us, reasons for disappearing...oh yeah, I know all about her stupid reasons. Her reasons for being so selfish and wanting to be alone. She quit riding with Anna and me. We can't even get her to go see Spirit. She quit everything with us."

"Sarah, I will not hear anymore of this. Do you understand me?"

"Yes sir, but you can't make me like her," and she sulked off.

"Where does she get that temper from?" Nicholas asked himself.

Sabotaged

Park received a call from work a few weeks after settling in her new home. She responded to her code name. She agreed to do it since it would be fast and easy. She had to drive to a resort some fifty miles up the coast to tag a courier for some black market weapons. It was a simple routine and would be over in a couple of hours. There was no risk of any danger.

She reached the assigned resort within three hours, and waited for three hours more, but the courier in question never surfaced. She waited another hour before deciding the assignment was a bust and heading to headquarters to debrief.

The elevated road followed a beautiful mountain along the ocean's edge. Not many tourists cared to hike their way to this stretch of the ocean, because access was not easy.

The warm wind blew Park's hair in complete

disorder, as she immersed in thought about how to get Sarah to stop being angry with her. If they were going to start over, she had to forgive her mother and come home.

Suddenly, an explosion in one of her tires blew her daughter from her thoughts. The impact threw her from the Jeep. The unmanned vehicle rolled down the incline and exploded upon impact.

She did not have time to think. The way the tire exploded did not feel like a blowout. The tires were practically new. There was no reason why it should have blown, unless someone helped it along. Someone had deliberately sabotaged her.

Park lay still for only a second before crawling on her belly to a culvert pipe further down, while confusion of the explosion was in the air. She hid quietly in her cramped position, while a vehicle drew to a stop somewhere above her for a short period and then started and faded into the distance.

The courier must have spotted her. If the would be

assassin was watching, it would behoove her for them to think they succeeded, so while the rescuers thought she died in the explosion, she contemplated her next move.

While waiting for the cover of darkness to fall around her, she heard sirens and people scurrying around the wreckage. Periodically, someone would yell a question or comment to another, yet she remained hidden and silent.

After the sky darkened and the tide drifted back out, she crept down the slope to escape down the beach. During the incident, she tore her dress in several places and lost one of her shoes. Sliding off the other shoe, she inched her way down the rocks. Once on solid sand, she began jogging, staying as close to the landline as she could. Her body was hungry, sore, and worn.

She was not sure who had tried to kill her, but if it had been this courier, he might have done his homework and be watching the people she would contact. Richardson was the only one she would trust. He would know how much danger she could be in, since it was his assignment.

Making the call without anyone seeing her was going to be hard, but she managed. "Richardson," he answered.

"Mr. Richardson, this is Maggie Evans, I am calling in reference to a, Park O'Ryan, you have working for you."

He responded to her code, "I am sorry; Mrs. O'Ryan was killed in an auto accident yesterday. Can I help you?"

"Yes, I heard the funeral was to be held at eleven ten at the Tide's Edge Mortuary," she coded.

"Right, uh-hmm"

"Is Mr. Summerville going to officiate?" she had given him her location.

"I believe Mr. Connors is, were you a friend of hers?" he coded in return.

"There was no one I trusted more than her. Thank you sir, you have been most helpful." Park hung up the phone.

The Mystery Begins

Less than two hours later, Nicholas came upon a sleeping Park hiding under a vacant rental house out of sight. He silently drew up to awaken her, only to face a gun as his greeting.

She released her aim, "Sorry about that. I was not sure who was sneaking up on me," she started.

"What is going on here? Richardson told me to come here and pick someone up and make sure no one saw me."

"I went to the Hanover resort to tag that stupid courier for the black market weapons, and he never showed his face. As I was leaving, somebody shot out my tire. My Jeep went over the mountain and blew."

"I may be wrong, but I don't believe there was an assignment for tagging a courier." Nicholas offered, "Come on, we will meet up with Richardson at rendezvous point and find out for sure." Her bare worn feet and tattered dress cried out for help, so he gave her his jacket to wear. "Park, you need to know something," he started, but she could see the expression was reverting to a personal nature.

"Nicholas, someone is out to kill me. We need to go. Nothing else matters," she prevented him from continuing.

Frustrated that the first time she had even talk to him since his admission, she would not even let him exonerate himself. He placed himself on his bike angrily, and she put her arms around his waist as they began their journey. He must find a way to tell her that Tessa had lied. He could not let her go on thinking that he was still carrying on with this other girl.

Shortly, they pulled up at a foreign apartment on the outskirts of Charleston. When the two dismounted the bike, while watching for prying eyes, Richardson was waiting for them.

"Care to tell me what is going on?" he asked, after securing the room.

Park replied, "Per your instructions, I went to the Hanover resort to tag Greigman, and he never showed. I waited for four hours and was heading back to report, when someone shot out my tire. I assume it was Greigman."

"I never sent you on any assignment," protested the boss man. "You told me you were retired. Why would I disrespect that decision? Who called?"

She answered, "I assumed it was Vanessa. She gave me all the details I would need over the phone."

"Vanessa never called. She is out on another assignment. She is not even in the country." He thought aloud, "If it is Greigman, he may have someone working on the inside, or else he has access to our procedures. My question is why? The man does not even know of your existence. We have not matured that assignment. It will be another week before we are ready to progress."

"I am sure Park has made some enemies along the way, sir," interjected Nicholas. "We need to look over the past assignments and see who might want her out of the way." This was the first he had heard of her retiring, but he could not stop to fret over that now.

"Gorshev is dead. He is the only one I know of that would have a price on her head," continued Richardson. "I will go back to the office and pull up back files and research. O'Ryan, you stay here and watch her."

"Sir, if someone is watching, they will get suspicious if Nicholas disappears all of a sudden. He has to go back and act normal. I can take care of myself," argued the target.

"You are right, but until I get back with the data, he will be fine here. O'Ryan, go get her some clothes to wear. She will want to clean up. Buy some men's clothes so it won't look suspicious. Park do you mind?"

"No sir, but really, I am perfectly capable of staying here alone."

He ignored her, "I'll be back ASAP. Get some food

in her."

"I bet you are hungry," Nicholas commented after Richardson disappearance.

"I have not had anything since yesterday morning," she admitted, as she drank a glass of heavenly water.

"I am going for food first. Lock the door behind me."

Park took this time alone to wash her face. The warm soapy water was soothing to her scrapes. Her ejection from the Jeep left her with only a few scrapes and bruises, a messed up shoulder, and scorned pride.

She fell into a chair and was almost asleep when Nicholas tapped on the door. She carefully peered to see if it was he before unlocking it.

Growing Suspicions

After satisfying their hungry bellies, they cleaned up the mess. It was not until then that Nicholas summoned up the courage to try again. "I have not been with Jankowski since that one night while you were gone."

"I know." She offered nothing else.

"I don't want you to think I would ever..."

Park interrupted him, "I do not think anything, Nicholas. I know you have been faithful since I came back. Don't worry over it anymore."

"I will worry until you promise me you will not let anything she says bother you."

"What makes you think she would say anything to me? I don't even know the girl that well." She changed the subject, "How is Sarah? Is she still angry with me?"

"Sarah is not mad at you. She is pouting because she

didn't get her own way. She will get over it soon enough. She loves and misses you very much." He encouraged.

"I think I will go take a shower now. I have a lot of dirt on me."

"I will get you some clothes. There is a store next block over."

When he placed the purchased clothes on the bed and shut the door behind him, he could still hear the shower. Richardson returned with a coded knock. He drew Nicholas away from the closed door to talk without being heard.

"Did you find anything?"

Richardson was hopeful, "It wasn't Greigman. He has been out of the country for the last week. It is highly possible that I found out who is responsible though. You did a job in Prague about two years ago with a man named, Echovich." Nicholas nodded. "We let him go, because he proved useful to us in the future. It is probable that he has tried to extract revenge on Park for bringing his operation down."

"How sure are you that he is our man?"

"Quite. He has gone underground here in the States over the last couple of days. He is listed black out with our sources. I have ordered an assignment to find and get him again. Do you want to lead it?" asked the protective boss.

"When and where?"

"Five minutes ago. Get going. I'll fill Park in."

Park had spent as much time in the shower as she dared. She did not want to leave its hot massaging pleasure.

When she did exit the bathroom, she was relieved to find that Nicholas had gone. She did not know how many more private meetings with him she could stand.

Richardson filled her in with the information. She

protested his captivity. "People will get suspicious if you are not at your normal post. You go on back, I promise, I will be fine."

"Can I not take a few minutes off for once? I am at that job the majority of my life, and it will not kill them for me to spend one afternoon with my best agent."

He smiled because his ruse had worked in making her feel sorry for him. Park placed a kiss on his cheek and a hug around his neck. "Yes sir, take all the time off you want. You will get no complaints from me."

He waited for Park to fall asleep right before dark, before the top agent decided to leave. Something in her subconscious woke her early the next morning, causing her to pull a gun on the intruder.

Relentless

"Is this becoming your way of greeting?" A prepared Nicholas disarmed her.

"Is this becoming your way of entering a room?" she returned.

He wanted to laugh, but felt restrained. "Touché. I came to take you home."

"Did you catch him?"

"A while ago."

Their conversation fell strained after that. It would be wonderful to go home, but she would rather anyone be with her than Nicholas. She still was unsure of what to say to him. Time away had not made the words come easy.

He hustled her to the door. The cool air outside burned her scratched face, but revived her spirit. She leaned her head back to allow the wind to blow her mind clean from all worry.

Before long, he deposited her inside her loft. "Would you like some coffee?" she offered out of politeness.

"No thank you. I have to get some sleep. I am dog tired."

She could no longer hold her emotions. The last little while came to a full head, and she felt that if she did not laugh she would cry. She burst forth in laughter, "Good, because I don't have any to make." Nicholas joined in her hilarity.

His phone rang, at that time, interrupting the harmony. "Yes?" he responded, "I see. Are you sure? Now what? Sure." Turning to Park after hanging up, he continued, "That was Richardson. Echovich was not responsible for your attack. He had proof of his whereabouts at the time of your attack. It is too late to get you back to the safe house unseen. Whoever is after you has probably already found out you are still alive."

"Where is Sarah?" panicked the mother.

"She should be at school, why?"

"I just have this feeling that she is in danger."

Nicholas took turn to panic. "I will call the school." After dialing and ordering that no one was to pick up Sarah except him or Park, he turned to the woman he loved. "I am going to get you and Sarah somewhere safe. How about the yacht? Out on the open water, you can see someone coming for miles. No one can get to you without your knowledge. I will set some guards to watch you and Sarah at a safe distance. I cannot lose her too."

"Sounds like a plan. Come on," ordered the nervous mother. She wanted to hurry and get to the school to ensure that Sarah was safe. She could not shake a feeling that her daughter was in danger.

They had to run by the house to swap the motorcycle for the truck before getting Sarah. The two parents extricated their daughter and headed for the yacht.

Sarah was confused and asked many unanswered questions. She knew her parents would not have taken such extreme measures if it were not a serious matter. However, she growled when she found Daddy was not coming with them. She was not ready to forgive Mom for separating them again.

Nicholas kissed his daughter and told her to, "be safe". He wanted to reach for his estranged wife and kiss her to be safe as well, but thought better of it.

"We have to get some supplies before we set sail," theorized Park to her begrudging daughter after Nicholas left. "We can run to the dock store and get a few necessities and be back in a jiffy."

They made a hasty supply run and then sailed out until the coastline was no longer in sight. Park anchored *Freedom's Park* and set plans to fix her daughter's supper. She was already feeling safer and calmer.

Sarah sulked at her captivity on the top deck watching her mother skillfully maneuver the tub. She wanted to convey to her mother just how angry she was; therefore she would not let her know she was enjoying this time with her. She defiantly marched down below when her mother told her to clean up for supper.

Darkness began enveloping them on the endless waters. Soon the darkness would reflect a silver ribbon donated by a beautiful moon, unfitting for the mood of everyone.

Park laid their small bounty on the deck table. Everything was waiting on Sarah. Why did she not come back? "Sarah! Supper is ready. Come on," she yelled below.

She stepped across the deck to deal with the metal part of a rope that was beating on the mast. She began getting agitated, because Sarah still had not come up. "Sarah!"

"Here she is Mommy Dearest. Sorry it took her so long to get ready. She sort of got tied up a little." Tessa Jankowski held her daughter with hands tied behind her back while brandishing a gun over her head. Sarah's face was bleeding. "I see you survived the crash. I am not surprised. Richardson told everyone you were killed. He almost had me convinced, when we brought in Echovich as the suspect. You don't think I am going to fail at my private mission do you?" A demonical smirk conquered her lips.

Tessa Jankowski had spotted Nicholas and Park from her watch at the school and followed them to the marina. When Park and Sarah went for supplies, she stowed away to await the right time to exact her revenge.

Fighting for Their Lives

Park had to think quickly. She was not going to watch another child gunned down at the hands of a lunatic. "Think O'Ryan!" She commanded herself.

Sarah held pleading in her eyes. Like her mother, she refused to cry. She would not give this woman the satisfaction of success.

"There is no need to bring Sarah into this. This is between you and me. If you want me, you have me, but leave her out of this."

The wicked sneered, "Oh I don't think so. As long as you and this little brat are around, Nick will never feel free to come to me. I have thought this out. Little Princess, is going to have a swimming accident, right before this boat blows to kingdom come."

"If you think this will get Nicholas to love you, you are mistaken. He loves Sarah more than anything in this world and would hate you forever," stalled the mother while coming toward the duo slowly.

"As if I intend to let him know I had anything to do with this. On the contrary Mommy Dearest. After all these years of abuse, poor little thing finally flipped her lid and did the horrific murder/suicide."

Park had a deaf cousin for whom she had learned and taught her girls sign language. She signed to Sarah to elbow the woman as hard as she could in the stomach and knock the gun out of her hand as soon as her mother was close enough to help.

Sarah watched her mother inch closer while frightfully waiting for the signal. She was proud of her mother in spite of her anger. Her mom could beat anyone that came along.

"Stop right there," ordered Jankowski. "I'm not as stupid as you think. Get over there and lower the life boat." Park obeyed. "Now Sarah, tell Mommy Dearest goodbye," she checked her watch. "Never mind. I don't have time, she's going to blow! Get to the edge!"

"Now!" yelled Park who covered the woman in a matter of seconds.

Sarah took her tied fists and hit Jankowski's face with all her power, then immediately knocked the gun out of her hand. Her superhero mom took over the fight.

She put the woman unconscious with one hit. Quickly, she untied Sarah's hands. "Go! Here," she ran to the stern and came back, "take the flare gun. Get in the lifeboat and row as hard as you can. Get as far from here quick."

"No Momma! Come with me," she cried hysterically with a squeaky voice.

"Listen to me. Get off this boat now! I have to try to diffuse the bomb. When you get a safe distance, send a flare up. Don't waste time doing it before. Go! Go!"

"Momma, I'm sorry about what all I said. I love you and I want you around, please," she could not stop the tears now.

"I know Honey, but please go. I will be all right. Just go, now! Momma loves you more. Now go." She pushed Sarah over the edge in the small boat.

She waited long enough to ensure Sarah was rowing and ran downstairs, with the ten-year-old's pleas resounding in her ears.

Park knew there was no way she could carry Jankowski in the water very far, so she would have to diffuse the bomb. She searched every nook and cranny to find it.

Tessa met her with a club as she came out of the kitchen, but the club hit the doorjamb. They struggled briefly. Park was still recuperating from the last mission and could not put her best foot forward, but it was enough to knock her nemesis out again.

This search revealed the explosive in the engine room. Thirty-eight seconds remained. There was no time to learn how to diffuse it.

She ran for all her might, placed Jankowski on her shoulders and proceeded to the edge of the yacht. She was about to jump, when the impact of the explosion threw Park and her load into the depths of the sea. The blast of the cold water awakened the sleeping figure who continued to struggle with her captor.

A Mother's Rage

Park saw that Jankowski had found some driftwood. She must keep up with her. If Tessa caught up with Sarah, she would kill her.

It seemed like they drifted in the water for hours before they heard a motor. A search light found its way to the swimmers.

Nicholas had decided to stay on the watch boat that night. Needing some sleep, he went to the lower bunks to rest. When they witnessed the explosion, Flannigan went below to wake him with the news.

As the guard boat sped across the distance toward the burning float, Nicholas held a vague hope that wife and daughter had survived. Relief overcame him when he saw two swimming figures, thinking it was his two most precious.

Strong hands pulled a weary Park to the safety of the boat, and she smiled her thanks at Flannigan, her rescuer. Nicholas pulled Jankowski from the water's depth, thinking that it would be Sarah.

The mother searched the deck for her daughter, "Did you not pick up Sarah? She was in the lifeboat."

Realizing whom he had pulled to safety, Nicholas searched the waters around them for a third swimmer. "I thought she was with you."

"I sent her with the flare gun in the life raft."

Henry stepped up, "I thought I saw a flare go off about the time of the explosion. I just thought it was been part of the explosion. It may have been a little west of here."

"Find her!" ordered a distressed mother.

The authorities took Jankowski below in handcuffs. The worried mother scrutinized the blackness surrounding their ship to find one sign of her child.

Shortly, she rejoiced to lift her cherished daughter onto the rescue boat, while the rest of the crew pulled up the lifeboat. She fell to her knees to search Sarah for injuries.

She worried, "Are you hurt? What did she do to you? You were so brave."

"I'm okay, Momma. She hit me a couple of times, but it didn't hurt too bad. I thought you were going to die." She embraced her mother as tightly as she could.

Park lifted her daughter in her arms and faced Nicholas with a fire in her eyes he had never seen. "How dare you bring this upon our child? What you do to me is one thing, but when you bring Sarah into it, it is unforgivable."

Nicholas watched her take their daughter away. His countenance fell. He had been responsible for putting both of their lives in danger. No matter how much he tried to protect them after the fact, it did not change the fact that he was responsible for the danger in the first place. The lust of the flesh will not go unpunished for a child of God. He only chastises those who are His. Park exposed to him how he could not have hurt her more if he tried.

I Surrender All

Pop enveloped both daughter and granddaughter tightly when they were safe at home. He had not known that his two little girls had been in danger until it was over. They had come to prove to him that they were safe.

This was the first opportunity she had to discuss her plans with Sarah. This would be a perfect chance to tell her and Pop together.

"Sarah," started her mom, "I have one more assignment to do, and then I am retiring to stay home with you. It is not a dangerous or long assignment, so you have nothing for which you should worry. When I get back, I thought we could find a place somewhere far away, settle down, and try to live a normal life. Would you like that?"

"You really mean it, Momma? No more leaving?"

"No more leaving after this assignment," smiled the mother, with an embrace for Sarah. "I have talked to Mr. Richardson, and he has officially retired me. My last assignment is for a friend."

Sarah frowned, "But what about Daddy?"

Park recovered the best she could, "Dad has his job, Honey. We cannot ask him to give everything up and move. He has his own life to live. You can spend as much time with him as you want, though. He loves you and will want you all the time."

Sarah thought things might have changed. She sadly replied, "I'll go with you, Momma."

Pop offered, "And you can always come see your grandpa. You can't leave me in the cold."

"Oh, Grandpa you are so silly. You could come live with us if you wanted to."

"She is right, Pop. Just move your new bride with us," laughed Park. "You are always welcome to visit any time for as long as you want."

Martha came in from the telephone, "Park, that was

267

Shawn. He said he had been trying to get a hold of you for days. Will you call him? He said it is important."

Sarah looked at her mom. Park smiled at her, "It is okay, Honey. That is the last job in which I told you. Dad will pick you up later, but I have to go, for now. It will be the last time."

"Momma," Sarah gripped her mother, "I love you."

"I love you too, Angel. Think about where you want to live while I am gone. We can go anywhere."

"What about Montana?" she suggested.

"Montana is perfect, but you do know we are starting over. We will not be staying at the old cabin."

Sarah crossed her arms. "Then I don't want to go to Montana."

"Well, you have a couple of weeks to figure it out. Goodbye everyone."

The Final Rescue

Shawn had called to announce that the rescue mission was scheduled. The old troop had been training for weeks, now. Park did request that Shawn include Nicholas in the rescue. Much as she was angry with him, she still trusted him with her life.

However precise the team may have been, the rescue was in vain. There were no POWs in the camp as thought. The years of research had served no purpose.

The ground team consisted of Creasman, Weasel, Park, Shipman, and Nicholas.

Duncan and Shawn were the pilots of this mission. Weasel and Shipman loaded up with Duncan during the egress route, while a paranoid Creasman followed Park and Nicholas into Shawn's.

A secondary mission included Park parachuting down to another territory to explore another possible camp. Shawn and Park were the only ones privy to this information. Since Creasman ended up on their chopper, Shawn was unable to fill Nicholas in on the details of this extra mission.

Over the appointed area, Park readied her descent, while Creasman watched with a scowl of curiosity. It was time. Shawn lowered the aircraft to the appropriate altitude, and Park made her jump.

Nicholas didn't have time to wonder why she jumped, because Creasman aimed his firearm and shot. He was going to show that girl what it was like to be in this war for real, no more pretenses of heroics. Nicholas pounced on the brute, shouting at Shawn for answers.

Shawn knew, once the plan was in motion, Park would not turn back for anything, so he kept flying. He circled around to make sure Creasman had not hit her.

Unloading at the point of return, Shawn took Nicholas to his hotel room. "She is going to another camp about twenty miles up. We think there may be some prisoners there. She is only scouting it out, and we rendezvous tomorrow at o six hundred."

"Why did she not say something before?" demanded Nick.

"It was top secret. She didn't want anyone to stop her. Kincaid doesn't even know."

"What do you plan on doing about Creasman? He is a loose cannon."

Shawn sighed, "I know. I knew he disliked Park, but I never thought he would go as far as that. They told me his wife left him for a scoundrel while he was serving his country. She didn't even give him time to die, before she up and left. Ever since he found out, he has had issues with women. He needs help."

"I am going with you tomorrow," stated Nicholas as he exited. "Take care of Creasman, or I will."

Six o'clock the next morning, the helicopter lay in wait for the expectant arrival. Six o'clock that evening, it was still in wait.

"Something has happened to her," worried Nicholas.

"She is a strong woman. She will make it." Shawn hoped in his heart that his words were true.

"What if Creasman hit her, and she is lying out there dying?" questioned Nick.

"She was to leave her radio at an egress point in case of trouble. I spent the night in the chopper, and she never called," informed the leader.

Nicholas raised his brows to this information, "You are in love with my wife, aren't you?"

Shawn started, "What makes you ask that?"

"I lost my memories, not my sight. I can hear it in your voice and see it in your face. You are in love with her," he accused again.

"Nick, old buddy, she is an impressive woman. I would be insane not to be in love with her, but I respect her marriage and her love for you. You don't have to worry about me trying to make the move on her." He was silent for a while, and then added, "I will forewarn you, though. If you don't reconcile with her, and she gives me the slightest chance, I am not going to pass it up."

Nicholas admired his bold honesty but disliked him because of his love for Park. Nonetheless, he did make it clear to Nicholas that they could not keep living like this. It was time for major changes. Either she would have to marry him and be a family, or he would have to burn her out of his heart forever.

Twenty-four hours of waiting brought no word from the huntress. Both men were concerned, but neither would suggest leaving, so they stayed for two more days. Their food supply was low and neither had much sleep.

The noon hour was upon them and Nicholas continued to pray silently. "Bring her back to me, if it be Thy will. I will make her mine. I will make her happy and proud to be my wife, if You give me another chance. I will not make the same mistake I made before. Please God, if it be Thy will."

"You sure pray a lot, Nick. Do you really think He is going to bring her out?" asked a skeptical Shawn.

"I have no doubt about it." The handsome man's jaw tightened under the conviction of his words.

Shawn could not help seeing what Park found irresistible in this gentleman. He was handsome and his character was pleasant. His quiet strength was alarming.

Nicholas added, "Park is strong, God will protect her. She will be back."

"She *is* strong. My father respected her greatly. He said it had been her plan to get me out of the prison camp. She willingly put herself in there to bring us out."

"I should know that, but I don't have that memory. There are so many that I do not have. It is frustrating for everybody to know everything about you except you."

Shawn took pity on the man. "I couldn't imagine what that is like. She really loves you Nick, old friend. She could never feel about me the way she does you. You are a lucky man."

Nicholas shook his head sadly, and they sat in silence until Nicholas broke it, "How long will you wait for her?"

"I am going to give her till sundown and then I am going in search of her. I think…we should have… gone…Did you hear that?" Shawn listened carefully.

"Land Rover to Red Baron," they faintly heard.

"I heard it!" shouted Nick.

"Land Rover to Red Baron." It came again.

Shawn picked up the radio, "This is Red Baron, come in Land Rover."

Silence.

"Red Baron to Land Rover, Land Rover, are you there?" He looked at Nicholas. "That is her." He pressed the button again, "Land Rover are you there?"

The response was a man's voice in the native tongue.

Rescuing the Rescuer

Nicholas sank. They must have grabbed her. He listened to Shawn carry on a conversation in the foreign language, and then he heard Park's sweet blessed voice. His heart turned tumultuous.

"Red Baron, this is Land Rover, about ten hounds are on the fox's trail, and the fox is triple cargo kangaroo. En route to rendezvous."

Shawn responded, "Land Rover, what hole is the fox in?"

"Negative. Drop point ten minutes ago. Maybe eight more miles."

"The horses will relieve the riders," Shawn ordered.

Her voice was weak, "Negative, Rabbit season is not in. Safer for rabbits to stay in the hole. Out."

Shawn saw Nicholas's searching eyes, "Want to go rescue her?"

He did not need to say more, Nicholas followed. "Is she okay?"

Shawn called back, quietly, "The man with her said she was pretty sick. That is why he got on the radio. There are three prisoners with them. We have about a five mile jog to meet up with them."

"I thought she was supposed to explore only?" came back Nick.

"They captured her and brought her to the prisoners. There were only three of them. That is all I know, except they have ten guards on their tails."

Nicholas prayed fervently. "Please let us make it in time, if it be Thy will, Lord."

He had pieced enough of Park's conversation together to understand that triple cargo meant three men accompanied her, and kangaroo meant one or more were injured and riding piggyback. He had to reach them before the guards did. Shawn was light on his feet, swift as a deer and the two made good time.

Shawn spotted movement ahead and motioned for Nick to take cover until they could see if it was Park. It was! They ran to meet her. Park was carrying a shell that used to be a man on her shoulders, and two pitiful American soldiers, painfully ran behind her the best they could.

When Shawn relieved Park of her load, they could see that her shirt was bloody and her wrists were bleeding. Her bruised face swelled her eye. She was burning with a fever.

She grabbed another soldier and helped him run, but Nicholas lifted her in his arms and ran for her life. She was a light load and they could go faster except the two prison-freed soldiers were weak and injured.

The journey to the chopper seemed longer and longer, until finally it came in sight. Nicholas and Shawn laid their loads inside. While Shawn went to pilot, Nicholas helped the other two in. The mighty wings began to whir.

The strongest looking prisoner was shouting, but it was not English. Nicholas looked to Shawn for translation. "He said she is infected with a fever. They brought her in with a wound, and would not help her."

Park's burning eyes looked into Nicholas's. "It is okay now," he was saying to her. "They are all safe." This seemed to ease her brow. Nicholas held her to his breast. She was burning up. He went to the medicine kit and found a cloth. Soaking it in some water, he placed it on her head. She thanked him with her smile.

"Nicholas," she mumbled feverishly. He bent closer. "I love you."

When they landed in Corpus Christy, Nicholas wasted no time in getting Park to the hospital. She had a gun shot wound in her shoulder, thanks to Creasman. Once the antibiotics made her sane again, she explained to them what she could remember.

Her wounded shoulder had not slowed her down, but the buzzards had announced an intruder. The filthy old betrayers soared overhead, tattling of her whereabouts shamelessly. The fire in her shoulder burned relentlessly.

Once the captors found her, they threw her in the dirt pit. They were nervous about an American penetrating their boundaries. They probably would not have been that suspicious of her had she not been shot.

The first two days they had beaten her, trying to gain information as to how and why she came into their camp. Of course, she would not even give them her name. They were going to kill her, when they discovered infection had set in.

When one of the guards tried to force himself on her, it gave her the opportunity to break free. She reached her bound hands around his drunken neck, quickly snapping the life from him. She procured his weapon first, and then used his knife to free her hands.

She stealthily worked her way back to the prisoners and took four more lives by knife in the process. The early hours of the morning provided her with a darkness that kept her hidden.

She was able to free all five men without notice. They were almost to safety when two guards spotted them. The locals managed to kill two of the prisoners during the escape. Park had given each one a weapon she had confiscated from the dead guards, and together they killed as many guards as possible before fleeing.

Will You, Will You Not?

Park O'Ryan had fought her last battle. Her youth was spent and it was time to take the remnants of her family and live life safely and completely. It did not matter where they lived. The world was their oyster.

Pop and Martha received a call from the son, telling of their return home in a few hours, which was enough time to gather all the friends. Nicholas flew Park home on Shawn's plane, where she was at his mercy since her jeep was gone.

The first thing she desired to do was to see her precious Sarah. Nicholas gladly drove her to the house, where Sarah greeted her with glee. She held back when she saw the bandages on her wrists and the sling on her shoulder. To make it unanimous, she was ready to give up this life to ensure her mommy never got hurt again. Deep down she hoped her dad would find a way back into their home.

All of the Claytons, Pop, Martha, and Fred greeted the prodigal friends with a little party. Bruce held on to his old friend for a long time refusing to let her go.

"Take a walk with me, Friend?" Bruce offered Park his arm.

Park kissed Sarah's hair. "Sweetie, we will be back in a little while. Are you ready to go home?"

Sarah suddenly looked so much older to her mother. She had grown up too fast. A passing regret crossed Park's lips in a kiss. Sarah responded maturely, "Yes ma'am. I will get my stuff." Sonya took her hand, and the two ran up the stairs with Matt following the best he could.

"Sarah tells me the two of you are moving away," Bruce became serious as they walked down the beach.

"It is true. It is about time I started thinking about her, and fulfilling her needs. It is time to retire and let someone else take up the sword."

"You are really leaving me?" He was not smiling anymore.

Tears began to run slowly down Park's cheeks, "You have been such a wonderful brother to me. I do not know if I can live without you, but I know I have to go for Sarah's sake. I cannot live like this anymore, Bruce. If I had listened to Matt and done this when he was alive, I would still have my Anna."

Bruce had tears on his face also, "You know, this will be the first time since we were ten, that we have been apart? I am going to miss my best friend."

"Come with us!" she smiled through her tears. "There will be plenty of room for everyone. We can find a secluded place far away and never have to fight battles again."

"I wish I could. I will be eligible for full retirement in a few more years. Maybe I will look you up then, and Christy and I will come to live wherever you are. Have you any idea where you are moving?"

"Not a clue. You will let Sonya and Matt come and stay with me in the summers, right?"

He had his hands thrust in his pockets while looking over the ocean. "Park, what am I going to do without you? You have been such an important part of my life. I love you so much."

"I know you have family ties that bind you to this place, but I do not. I cannot breathe here. I have to go. I have been thinking about Matt a lot lately, and I do not like what I have thought. He wanted me to retire when Anna was born, but I selfishly cast his wants away. I know Anna is with her Daddy in heaven right this moment, but I will have to face him some day with what I let happen to his little baby. Please try to understand."

"I do understand. I guess I was being selfish myself."

"I love you, you big lug."

They fell into a long embrace.

"Am I interrupting," Nicholas asked quietly, and the two separated and quickly wiped away the tears.

"No Brother, we were just saying our goodbyes. She is all yours," Bruce held out his hand for Nicholas to shake.

Nicholas waited until Bruce was out of hearing range before beginning, "Park, I know I have let you and Sarah down. There are no words to say except I am truly sorry that I inflicted this pain upon you. I don't expect you to forgive me any time soon, but I pray you will someday."

She put her hand on his arm, "It is already done. That is ancient history. Think of it no more."

He tried to watch her eyes as he continued nervously, "Park, if you are looking for happily ever after, you can't find it except in fairy tales, but I would like to try to give you happiness for the rest of your life. I do need to know if I ever stand a chance with you." As Park began to respond, Nicholas put his finger to her lips. "Let me finish while I can. Tomorrow night I will be waiting at the Indigo House at seven o'clock. I want you to sleep on it, think about it, and come to me. Your attendance will validate that you will become my wife. Your absence will inform me to never bother you again. I love you, but I understand if you do not feel the same. If you are not there by seven, I will know your decision."

He did not give her the opportunity to respond before leaving her standing there with what he had said.

Failure to Launch

A huge tropical storm blew in Saturday with winds and rain gusting. Park answered the door at least twenty times for deliveries of daisies from Nicholas.

Meanwhile, Nicholas felt an answer to his prayer had come. God let her survive in the line of duty to come back to him. He believed God granted him this prayer. He did believe that this was the last chance he would ever have for a reconciliation.

Nicholas nervously prepared himself for her decision. He delivered an excited Sarah to Pop's house for the evening.

The rain did not hamper his handsome appearance. His neatly pressed black coat proudly rested on his broad shoulders. The white tie adorned his neck in splendor. In his anxiety, he arrived an hour early. Women ogled the gallant vision of the debonair man waiting at the table. He waited for his goddess to appear. His eyes searched every person coming through the door.

At seven thirty, Park had not come. His anxiety turned to despair. She was not coming. He had his answer, and she was not coming. She did not love him…but she did! She told him so in her delirium. His mind raced. She could not forgive him for putting Sarah's life in danger. His countenance fell. Eight thirty came and still no Park. She was not coming.

Nicholas jerked the bow out of his tie, as he slammed the back door to the brick beach house. He had ridden his motorcycle up the stretch of beach in the pouring rain, not caring whether his fine clothes were ruined or not. He walked into a banner and ripped it down with fierceness.

Bruce and Christy were in the process of preparing a congratulatory party, when he surprised them, "What in the world is wrong, Nick? Where is the bride?"

"Apparently, she made her choice," he growled, slumping into the den chair, while wiping the wet strand of hair from his forehead.

"I don't understand," said Christy.

Nicholas looked at her as if she were dumb, "She didn't show up. She would rather me stay out of her life for good."

Bruce jumped from the chair in which he had climbed to hang balloons. "When I talked to her earlier, she was excited about it. She had every intention of meeting you."

"She asked me which shoes she should wear when I called," interjected Christy.

"Then she changed her mind." scowled the rejected groom.

Bruce became concerned, "Something sounds fishy here. Nick, I know she was coming tonight. I talked to her about five thirty or six. Come on. We will check it out."

"You go. You are her best friend."

Bruce pulled him out of the chair by one arm, "Not this time. I am not going to let you be bullheaded this time. You will never know what happened, until you see for yourself." He pushed the belligerent Nick.

Bruce tried to remain cheerful for the ride over while Nicholas brooded. He should have known that she had moved on with her life without a second thought of him.

When they reached Park's building, both men took the stairs two at a time. Bruce rapped his knuckles on the door, but silence responded. A few seconds later, he repeated the rapping before dangling his keys to find the one to her apartment.

Though he said nothing, it annoyed Nicholas that she had given Bruce a key to her loft. First, he had a key to their house and now he has a key to her loft. He despised Bruce Clayton at this particular moment. Maybe Park was in love with Bruce. Maybe that was why she did not want him.

Bruce threw the door open and quickly glanced over the room. "Park?" He proceeded to the kitchen. "Park, are you here?"

Nicholas waited outside the door. He was going to simmer in his misery. He didn't want to find out that she really chose not to meet him.

Suddenly, heeding to Bruce's somber tone, he stepped inside and immediately forgot all of his ill thinking. Park lay on the blood stained wooden floor. Her white dress turned crimson, and the daisies in her brown curls soaked in a thick red substance.

Down for the Last Time

"Nick, call the ambulance."

He made the call to 911 and stooped over the seemingly lifeless body. "There is so much blood," he said.

Bruce calculated, "I talked to her a little after six, and it is 9:15 now. She could've been laying here for about three hours. That would explain the amount of blood. I hear the sirens. I will go direct them up."

"Honey, can you hear me," Nicholas called gently, "we are going to get you to the hospital, so hang on. I love you."

The paramedics lifted her easily onto their stretcher. The blood released part of its hold on her as the rain pelted against her pale flesh. She still looked lifeless lying there.

Bruce and Nicholas followed the ambulance to the hospital with worry on their brows. "Do you think she is going to be alright?" Nicholas wondered aloud.

"She will be fine. She is a tough cookie."

Several hours later, the doctor emerged from the double swinging doors and approached the nurse at the desk. She pointed toward the two men who had their heads thrust into their hands. Bruce rubbed his short buzzed hair and flung his body back into the chair, when he saw the doctor advance with his head shaking.

"Which one is Park O'Ryan's husband?"

"I am." Nicholas jumped up hopeful.

"What happened to her?" accused the doctor.

Both men looked puzzled until the doctor explained, "She has a broken rib, a punctured spleen, and damaged gall bladder. It looks like someone has been using her as a punching bag. Do you hit your wife, Mr. O'Ryan?"

Nicholas became enraged, "No, I do not."

"Then, what happened to her? It appears to have

happened over a little time. Has she been in a car wreck or something?"

Again, the two men just looked at each other. Nicholas asked, "How long would you say she has been like this?"

"Maybe a few days. She should have shown some signs." The doctor looked curiously at them, "I can remove the gall bladder with no repercussions, but the spleen has to heal itself. I will send out the proper papers for you to sign, Mr. O'Ryan." His accusatory tone informed Nicholas that he did not believe him.

One phone call from Bruce to his wife brought in the troops. They all gathered around while Park was in surgery.

Sarah climbed in her Daddy's lap and slept most of the night. She was not awake when the doctor came back out to report that all went well, and Momma was in recovery. Actually, she did not waken until the morning light shined in her eyes; then father and daughter went to see mother.

"I tried to come," the invalid mumbled at the sight of Nicholas.

"I know. It's all right," he kissed her forehead.

She had tears on her cheeks, "I tried to come. Did I lose my chance?"

"Honey," he kissed her tears, "I am right where I plan to be for the next fifty or sixty years. You cannot get rid of me. I know you tried to come, and just as soon as you are out of here, I am going to make you my bride, if I have to push you in a wheelchair."

She smiled weakly, "Sarah, my Angel, what are you doing here?"

Sarah imitated her mother in answering, "Momma, where else would I be?"

Nicholas left so that the rest of the gang could come in.

Bruce demanded, "Mind telling me how you broke that rib?"

She thought for a minute, "When I was on that rescue mission, one of those goons hit me with his rifle. I knew my side was bruised, but I didn't think it was serious."

"You didn't think it was serious?"

"No," she defended.

"Stubborn as a mule, Christy. I told you, she is as stubborn as a mule."

Going, Going, Gone

Although Nicholas did not remember it, Park wore the same silver gown and slippers she wore when she married him the first time and Bruce gave her away for the second time.

The groom stood in humble adoration as she came down to be his bride. She was the most incredibly beautiful woman he had ever laid eyes on.

The vows were traditional, but Nicholas added a quote from the Song of Solomon: the love story of beauty. *"Thou are beautiful, O my love, as Tirzah, comely as Jerusalem, terrible as an army with banners. Turn away thine eyes from me, for they have overcome me: thy hair is as a flock of goats that appear from Gilead: Thy teeth are as a flock of sheep which go up from the washing, whereof every one beareth twins, and there is not one barren among them. As a piece of a pomegranate are thy temples within thy locks. There are threescore queens, and fourscore concubines, and virgins without number. My dove, my undefiled is but one; she is the only one of her mother, she is the choice one of her that bare her. The daughters saw her, and blessed her; yea, the queens and the concubines, and they praised her. Who is she that looketh forth as the morning, fair as the moon, clear as the sun, and terrible as an army with banners?* Solomon must have been looking at you when he wrote that song, for it describes you perfect. And as long as I live, in this same mind, I will cherish you my love."

The charm claimed the smile of his most precious as she watched his eyes in faith. He had not thought it possible, but she was more beautiful with that charm in her smile. Oh, how his heart rejoiced!

Before the ceremony was complete, Nicholas requested they all join him in a prayer of praise to thank

299

God for His grace and mercy. After the prayer, the preacher finally allowed him to kiss his bride.

"Have you told her yet," asked Fred at the reception.

"No, but we will now." He held Park's hand in his arm, refusing to let it go for any reason. "Honey, thanks to our dear friend here, we will be moving to that solitude you desire. Remember the house in Maine? It is ours. We traded the Montana getaway for the lighthouse, and Fred is going to take over this house. It will work out wonderfully, will it not? Also, Bruce and Christy will get more use out of the North Carolina house than we would."

Park turned to her old friend and gave him an affectionate kiss on his cheek. "I will miss you my friend. You have been there for me always and I shall never forget that. I love you Fred."

"Ah Precious, you'll be coming to visit," he blushed, but he knew she would not be coming back to Charleston. He turned to Nick, "Uh, about that fist thing, I owe you an apology." Park looked at each of them curiously, but neither offered an explanation.

Nick slapped his back, "I thank you for it, Fred."

The hands clasped in a handshake, and Fred leaned to him, "Don't you hurt her again."

Shawn showed respect to Nicholas in his handshake. "Park, in another place and time, it would have been great. Congratulations Nick. Take good care of her."

Nicholas smiled his thanks.

Next, Richardson growled his congratulations to them. Truth was, he had already lost this daughter-like agent, but he was losing Nicholas as well. He was losing the two best agents he ever encountered. "That's what you get, you old fool, for getting mushy over them," he chided himself after Park gave him a last goodbye kiss.

Kathy, Bob, and the children were in line for their goodbyes as well. They promised to be there for Thanksgiving dinner, as usual. They wanted Nicky and Park to visit them soon, but Park made no promises.

301

"Martha and I volunteered to drive the horses up with Sarah," Pop kissed his daughter-in-law.

The bride waited to say her goodbyes to her oldest and dearest friend until last. How could she say her final farewells to her life support of all these years? The two hugged, cried, and stammered through the tears. Christy and the kids were in the huddle. "Goodbye old friend. Thanks for the memories," cried Bruce.

"I will see you and Christy at Thanksgiving. You will come up and be with us please? Our children cannot lose each other." She could not let go of this lifelong friend.

"It is a date," said Christy getting one last hug.

Park told Nicholas in his ear, "We have to go or I will not be able to leave, ever."

***

They flew the plane he had once given her as his first bride to their magical lighthouse, where the newly married couple sat on the edge of the tower watching God's handiwork.

Park held her husband's head in her lap, teasing his face with her fingertips, as the sun settled down over the ocean's edge. Nicholas reached his arms up around her, "I hope I can give you happily ever after. You certainly deserve it."

She bent to meet his lips, "You may not, but God has. He has blessed me beyond measure. Twice, He gave me your love. Happily ever after will come when we spend eternity in Heaven."

Made in the USA
Charleston, SC
13 February 2015